C0-ALZ-618

Our Father, Who Art in Cuba

Brian L. Kerr

Cover by
Tanya James

CANUSA BOOKS / CANUSA LLC

Brian Kerr/CANUSA LLC
Merida, Yucatan, Mexico

www.briankerrnovels.com

Publisher's Note: This is a work of fiction. Names, characters, places, and incidents are a product of the author's imagination. Locales and public names are sometimes used for atmospheric purposes. Any resemblance to actual people, living or dead, or to businesses, companies, events, institutions, or locales is completely coincidental.

Book design © 2013, BookDesignTemplates.com

Ordering Information: Special discounts are available on quantity purchases by corporations, associations, and others. For details, contact the publisher at the address above.

CANUSA LLC/Brian Kerr — First Edition

ISBN 978-0-9904179-9-6

Printed in the United States of America

Thanks to my wife Marla for being the inspiration for most of the little details in the book, and to my brother Wayne for his guidance and the suggestion that it was time to tell some of the stories of my twenty-five years of visiting Cuba.

Thank you, as always, to my talented baby sister Tanya James for the wonderful cover.

And thanks, most of all, to the friends, family and neighbors in Cuba for their courage and fortitude and for the fact that there has been so much more laughter than tears.

SANDRA

First Degree Burns

Life in Cuba wasn't all bad. There were lots of good things about it, too. Like, for instance, for people like Sandra who loved movies, there was Saturday night movie night. Fidel liked to do little things in defiance of the Yankees to the north, like the caricatures that always showed up in the Granma newspaper of the American presidents doing or saying something particularly imperialistic, or the big banner he had painted along the seawall in Havana that said, "Imperialist, we have absolutely no fear of you!" So stealing first-run movies and broadcasting them free to Cubans was by far her favorite thing about Fidel. That she had to watch the movies on a forty-year-old Russian television set that distorted the screen so tall people were short, and short people were laughable; well, that wasn't such a great thing.

Sandra loved the movies and the glamorous life she was sure all of the actors and actresses lived so much she had traded two crocheted sweaters, worth more than thirty dollars at retail price in the Candonga, where she worked, for the three-month-old movie magazine. So what if there was only about a dollar's worth of the cotton tobacco twine to make them both. She had spent more than a week crocheting the two sweaters, mostly after ten o'clock at night. When she'd seen the magazine sticking out of the tourist's hand-bag, she knew she had to have it, even if she had to clean out her six-foot wide stall made out of bent rebar and fishing net she had scavenged from her father.

The Candonga, as it was called, was the handcraft market the tour buses stopped at so visitors could buy typical Cuban crafts. It was called Candonga after the markets the Cuban soldiers frequented during the nasty war in Angola. Sandra's father had served there, but changed the subject every time she'd asked him about it.

Sandra had taken the magazine home that same afternoon and hadn't told anyone she had actually ironed it under a towel so that it looked new again. This particular issue was dedicated to Kevin Bacon, one of Hollywood's most-prolific actors, and a personal favorite of Sandra. She had studied the cover before ever turning a page. It had seemed so cool to her how Kevin and his wife, Kiera Sedgewick, seemed to jump right off of the page at her, their heads in front of the letters of "Hollywood Weekly", and there was a sort of shadow behind them that made them appear three-dimensional. When she compared it to the "Granma", with the bleeding black ink and faded pictures of smiling, happy farm workers, Sandra wondered what century she actually lived in.

She had debated waiting two days until Sunday to read it completely, but the temptation was too much for her. She had tried to go to sleep after crocheting until one in the morning, but the vivid colors of the front and back covers had been seared into her corneas, and they were all she could see when she closed her eyes. She could hear her mother and step-dad, Leonardo, and their incessant grunting and moaning, reminding her that she didn't have a man in her life; and her two-year-old half-brother, Leonardito, who had a sort of combination snore and whistle. Since her tiny transistor radio that the Italian tourist had given her a few months after she started in the Candonga had died a slow death, this was now the music of her life. The wind instruments consisted of the twenty-year-old fan that had a hitch when it got to the end of its cycle and made a little click as it jumped a cog. Add to that the flopping of the curtain against the aluminum window slats every time the breeze from the fan hit it. That old blue metal fan with one missing button was the only thing that had survived the marriage between her parents. The cheap plastic ones they sold now wouldn't be around by the time Leonardo got tired and left with the little tart she'd seen him leaning over a couple of weeks earlier. All he would leave would be another mouth to feed. The rhythm section consisted of the two different water drips from the bathroom and kitchen, and the horns and

4

trumpets came from the neighbor's cat that was constantly in heat, and the dogs of every shape and size that chimed in with her as she prowled the connected roof-tops. She usually avoided the roof of Sandra's house, since it was questionable whether it could sustain the weight of an adult cat.

The majority of Cuban homes are built as inexpensively as possible -- aside from being insanely expensive compared to the Cuban salary, materials were almost impossible to come by, unless, of course, you had the right connections and a car available to go and find them in the next city or even another province. Consequently, there was only one interior door in the house Sandra shared with her mother, and whomever was her mother's latest "love of her life". Leonardo was the third "true soul mate" since Sandra's father had gotten his teenaged fling knocked up when Sandra was only four years old. With the magazine resting under two volumes of the Russian encyclopedias in the living room next to the street, that meant Sandra needed to run the gauntlet of Leonardito's crib and the beast with the two backs, as someone had called it once. It was either that or go around the outside of the house, down the little alleyway, and scale the wall with the broken bottle security barrier, and then come in through the front door with the rusted hinges that made more noise than the neighbor's stupid rooster that couldn't tell time, crowing at all hours of the day and night.

At nineteen, Sandra knew she was way behind in Cuban culture. She should probably have two children, by two different fathers by now. Sure, she'd had a couple of boyfriends, and wouldn't class herself as an angel by any standard, but she figured there was plenty of time to enjoy life before cooking and cleaning and ironing for some guy who spent his days drinking cheap rum and playing dominos while she brought home the money from the Candonga. Nearly every woman in the market had the same story — "Why would he work in the sugar cane fields to bring home a hundred and forty lousy pesos a month when I can make that in a day here? Better he stay at home and take care of the house and the kids." Those were the same women who would cry on her shoulder about their surprise when they learned that "Harry Homemaker" was keeping busy with a neighbor's daughter while she was turning three shades darker in the sun.

And the music. Oh, how Sandra loved to dance and sing along to the music, especially Polo Montañez, the "Guajiro Natural" from Pinar del Rio, who had captured the hearts of every Cuban with his songs about life in the cane fields and sitting behind his horse on his carreton. Between Polo and Romeo Santos, her dream man with his romantic songs, she kept her friends in the Candonga entertained as she sang and moved her body just like the half-naked girls in the videos on television. She always giggled when she watched

6

the distorted bodies that looked more like chubby dough-boys on her screen.

Sandra opted for her regular method of averting her eyes and passing her mother's bedroom as quickly as possible on her way to the living room. She knew they'd been aware of her movements, because she felt the pause in the action, and knew Leonardo had looked back toward her. She didn't want her mother to be alone, but she sure wished she'd find a better companion than this guy. She didn't like the way he looked at her when her mother wasn't in the house, and he made comments that could be taken in more than one context, always keeping himself protected with a "she misunderstood me completely" excuse if she ever were to say anything. Aside from attending to her little brother, though, she tried to have as little contact as possible with her step-father. It was still uncomfortable, though, because she could never wear anything revealing, even in the house; she didn't want even the hint that she was showing him a sign. It was definitely time to have her own place, but the truth was she was the one who had paid for most of this house, and almost everything in it, with what she made in the Candonga.

In the refuge of her favorite wooden rocker, she clicked on the dim lamp she used to crochet with at night so it wouldn't bother the others who were asleep. It wasn't nearly bright enough to read comfortably with, but she would make do with it. She quietly slipped the magazine out from under the encyclopedias and breathed in the odor of the ink before opening it to the inside cover. There was an ad for the latest Adam Sandler movie, with Drew Barrymore, again. She had loved the previous one, where she lost her memory and he had to make her fall in love with him every day. Aside from seeing it one Saturday night on television, she had rented it and watched it over and over again one weekend on a borrowed DVD player. If she lived on her own, her first two pieces of furniture would be a color television and a DVD player.

Even the table of contents was beautiful to her: the font and the way it was placed over a collage of pictures of Kevin Bacon with different actors and actresses over what seemed to be a twenty five year span of time. She wanted to go straight to the article about him, but decided it was best to flip through every page, reading every word. She nearly forgot at first that the magazine was in English, and she had only rudimentary, "sell-to-the-yumas" English. "Beautiful crochet", and "I make" and "good price", probably wouldn't be found in the articles and advertisements. She didn't mind her lack of understanding of the writing, though. She was enthralled by the beautiful women and handsome, usually shirtless, men. The dresses they wore cost more than Sandra would make in a lifetime of selling crocheted clothing and sneaking pieces of illegal black coral necklaces and bracelets.

The article about Kevin Bacon, when she finally got to that section, was easier to figure out for her. She had heard the concept of six degrees of separation — the one that suggests that everyone on the planet can be connected within six degrees — someone you know or are related to would be considered first degree; anyone those people knew or were related to would be your second degree, and so on. There were graphs and lines connecting Kevin Bacon to at least a hundred different actors, living and dead, and it was difficult to reach a fourth degree. Even Lassie the dog was connected by the third degree. If she would have been visible in the dim light that night, there would have been a smile so peaceful and satisfied on her face that no one would guess there were forces that plotted against this sweet young woman.

When Leonardo walked into the living room at six in the morning, still in boxers and the cotton undershirt he seldom took off except to wash, he was surprised to find Sandra curled up in the rocker, the magazine still in her lap.

"You're up early," he burped out loud. She adjusted her position on the chair to provide less of a view of her long legs.

"Up late, actually," she corrected him. "I haven't been to bed."

"Your mother's still sleeping. You mind fixing me some eggs?"

Sandra bristled as she bit her tongue so she wouldn't remind him again she wasn't the help. She did more of her share of cleaning and cooking and taking care of little Leonardo, but that was because she felt a duty to her mother. Cooking a couple of eggs wasn't any big deal, and she could do it in five minutes, but the point was this guy was just another typical Cuban male, who thought every woman was born to serve him. He would rather die of thirst than get up from the table to pour himself a glass of water. And worse, her mother jumped up to get him his water, putting three pieces of ice in it, just the way he liked it, and apologized if she forgot to iron the right shirt or pair of pants so he could spend the day playing baseball and flirting with the high school girls who passed by the fire hall with their short skirts bouncing with the sway of their hips. She was sure the girl she'd seen him with the other night was a senior in the preparatory school down the street from the cemetery, a few blocks from her maternal grandfather's flower market.

She made a point of not jumping to her feet to comply with his request. She took time to return the magazine to its place between the encyclopedias and set the rocker back into its usual position, and then headed toward the kitchen. She knew he ached to remind her he was in a hurry to get to work, and deliberately stopped at Leonardito's crib to check on him and adjust the little blanket first. There hadn't been a fire in Trinidad since the German tourist found his wife in bed with her Cuban boyfriend and torched every square inch of the house. Leonardo would never have a moment's rest if every tourist who married a Cuban woman or man knew what really went on after they boarded their flight home to their country. One of her Aunt Ines' neighbors was married to an Italian man who came to see her for a month twice a year. He would work hard at home so that he could shower her with the luxuries she deserved — automatic washing machine, a big new color television, stereo system, and new cupboards. Every trip to Trinidad was a constant shopping spree. During that month, her Cuban husband stayed at his parents' home in Cienfuegos. Luckily for him, though, his German wife only came once a year. At that time, they would hide all of the new toys the Italian had paid for, so he could bleed as much out of the German lady as possible, while his Cuban wife used Italian money to rent a car and enjoy vacations at Cayo Coco, in Ciego de Avila. They didn't even try to hide their clever plan from the neighbors.

In the Candonga, almost every woman except Sandra was either married or had steady boyfriends. Like the American television series from the seventies, "Beverly Hillbillies", any woman not married with children by eighteen was either very ugly or must be a lesbian. Sandra was the Elly May of the Candonga. She had even heard the murmurs and suggestions that she must be on the other team from women who knew her well. Still, every time a new group of tourists passed through the market, Sandra saw the open flirting and batting of eyes, and even plenty of extended "tours" of the city. Most of the women she knew in the market would flat out leave their Cuban husbands without even a note if they got an offer from one of these tourists they didn't even know. The moral compass in Cuba was missing its true north.

In order to be considered married in Cuba, once Fidel had abolished religious practice, a girl needed to pack a bag of her underwear and toothbrush and sleep overnight with her boyfriend. Boom — married — let the ironing begin. Immediately, in order to cement the relationship, the girl should get pregnant and have his child — that would keep him faithful and happy. Right! More often than not, the fact that she gained weight during her pregnancy and lost her youthful body was reason enough for him to spend more time out with the boys, and if there was another young girl willing to sleep with him, well, what could that hurt? Crying babies could be a nuisance, and especially if he'd come home in the wee hours of the morning, smelling of perfume, and his wife had suddenly turned into some jealous, possessive, unattractive creature.

The good news? Divorce was even easier. Pack up her things, take them to her parents' house, and he could be at the disco by ten o'clock, free and single. Child support? In Cuba the only child support is the little wooden seat that is attached to the cross bar on a bicycle so that a baby can ride without falling off.

There were, of course, legal marriages in Cuba, with papers and ceremonies to prove it. For the most part, these were performed because there was some economic reason involved — usually property ownership. Things got very complicated in Cuba when it came to transferring ownership of properties, and that's where a marriage license could make or break a deal. Property ownership in Cuba was very cumbersome, to say the least, with buying and selling of properties not allowed. Properties could be traded for others of equal value for sake of convenience, so there were a lot of paper marriages performed in order to get the ownership of a house into the right hands. It was all a game — the government placed impossible rules, and Cubans found, or made, loopholes to jump through. Marriage was one way, and willing the property to another person was also a commonly-used method. Sandra's house, for example, was actually half of a house. A wall had been built down the middle of a large house that a nice lady named Juana owned. She was a widow with grown children who had homes of their own, so in order to meet her financial needs, she agreed to will the half of her house to Sandra, in exchange for an unspecified sum of money, which of course didn't show up on any documents. Juana's half included the kitchen and bathroom, so Sandra needed to figure out where to put these so that they wouldn't look like they were stuck on as an afterthought. Additional front and back doors were added, and voila — one house was now two. Juana had some money to fix the roof of her side of the house, and Sandra had a place to clean and to spend every dime she made in the Candonga. She immediately got her mother, Dalila, out of a bad situation by sending over a carreton moving crew to load up everything that was hers. She asked her Uncle Felix to pay a visit to the guy who thought he had the right to use his hands on her when she didn't go along with his drunken tirades. Having an uncle with a black belt in karate could be useful at times. Naturally, Dalila had wasted no time in finding a replacement for the jerk she'd left – she didn't like the idea of being alone.

The fact that marriage and divorce were so quick and easy in Cuba made for another particular phenomenon — half-brothers and -sisters everywhere you turned. "This is my half-brother on my mother's side, and I have a half-brother and -sister on my father's side," was so common in Cuba that family trees looked more like prickly pine bushes — there were branches going in every direction possible. It was most rare in Cuba to see a family with all of the children from the same father, and the father didn't have children with another woman from a previous marriage.

So when she had read the story about Kevin Bacon and how he could connect himself to every actor in Hollywood, Sandra had chuckled inwardly. Trinidad was a relatively small city of about fifty thousand, and was nearly five hundred years old. For reasons like not being able to buy and sell properties, moving from your birth city in Cuba was difficult and uncommon. That meant that there were only so many different families over so many generations in Trinidad. Sandra's own father, Ergeny, had four children with four different wives, so far, and by the looks of it he hadn't stopped his quest — his latest wife was only two years older than Sandra. The next one would surely be younger. Her mother now had another son from her latest "installment", and her half-brother Ergeny Junior had a half-sister. If she considered only her father as a first degree connection, the second degree was already connected to dozens of families, all of which were as fractured as her own. The fact that her father's latest wife was black made another entire section of the community connected to her. It was possible, she had thought, that there was no one in Trinidad who couldn't be connected to her by the third degree, and certainly by the fourth.

She had fallen asleep in the rocking chair going through a list of different people she could think of, no matter how far removed they were from her: the guy who delivered bread to the house in the morning -- married to a cousin of the girl in the next stall in the Candonga. The girl who took blood from her for her analysis the week before -- daughter of her father's ex-brother-in-law from his third marriage. No matter who she could think of, there was an easy connection. She had laughed out loud when she made the connection to a bird that she saw through the window -- cousin of the bird that the cat on the roof ate two days earlier.

Whether she had slept or not slept, Sandra needed to clean up and get ready to go to the Candonga — her crocheted clothing didn't sell itself, and now there were at least fifteen other women selling the same stuff as she did. What did the government care? As long as everybody paid their fees, they were happy. The real trouble began when the day of the "patente", or rent payment, was approaching and they needed to ensure they had the money in their hands on time. They had made a verbal pact not to lower the prices, but most of the ladies forgot about it when they saw the green bills in the hands of the Yumas. Sandra's stall was the last one, and that was normally the worst place to be. For some reason, though, week in and week out, Sandra sold more product than any of her fellow Candongereros...

She had a theory about sales she felt was paying dividends for her — she acted as though it didn't matter to her one bit if the customers bought from her or not, like she would be just as happy if they let her keep the sweater or girl's dress on her table. Other women practically begged the tourists to buy something, making up stories about their situation at home, that they needed their first sale of the day for luck, so they couldn't take no for an answer. Sandra's attitude was different — she had problems in her life like everyone else. Maybe not as serious as those with

16

sick children or relatives, obviously, but nobody in Cuba had enough of the things they needed, and there was always someone in the family in need of extra help. Before leaving her house for the long walk over cobblestone streets to the market, she had a ritual that she played out just for herself. She would look in the mirror on the wall of her bedroom — technically half a mirror, since it had fallen off and broken into two triangles when Leonardo had pushed the closet too hard up against the other side of the wall. The good news was, now both of them had a mirror in their rooms. She had to turn her face to an abnormal angle to fit it into the remnants, but she would make a point of confirming her "outside" smile was firmly in place, and any troubles she had in her life would stay inside the door to the house when she left. At the Candonga, she was carefree Sandra, enjoying the warm Cuban sun and visiting with the tourists. If they bought something, great; if not, great. More often than not, and certainly more often than with her fellow clothing saleswomen, Sandra sold one or two more pieces a day than anyone else, and at higher prices. She recalled the day, more than a year earlier, when a tourist from Spain who had been hanging around all afternoon taking pictures for some tour guide he was working on, had approached her.

"You must be happy because you sell so much," he had commented.

Without a moment's hesitation, Sandra had responded, "No sir, I sell so much because I'm happy." That was to be her motto in the market and in life.

Sure, she wished she had a more stable family life. She even still had a fantasy that her father would come back to the house and tell his mother that he'd made a big mistake, and wanted to come back home and be a family again. Not very likely, since there had been three other wives and countless other adventures since he'd left home to be with wife number two, already seven months pregnant with her half-brother Ergeny. Sandra wished more than once that she had been born a boy, so she could have been the one to carry their father's first name. She was so jealous of Ergeny Junior, looking exactly like their father, and even following him into the ocean. Some said the son was an even better diver than his father. Sandra couldn't confirm or deny that. She only knew she hadn't been born with the gene they shared.

Her father had asked her to join him once while he fished in the bay between Casilda and the Ancon Peninsula where the all-inclusive hotels were located. Sandra enjoyed snorkeling, and agreed to accompany him for a day. She had assumed the job of keeping track of the empty bottles that acted as floats where the fish her father harpooned hung in the water. Her father was so graceful as he took a deep breath, gave her a thumbs up signal, and almost slid down in the water near the rusting sunken ship. He moved effortlessly, obviously more at home in the water than on the surface. Sandra would always count, subconsciously, every time her father went under. She knew there were times when she got to two hundred before he emerged, lifting up two or sometimes three fish. She would haul the floating bottles over to where he was, and he would tie them on and smile at her.

She wanted to hate him – he had all but destroyed his mother's life, and hadn't ever even bothered to show up for any of her birthdays or school functions. But when he smiled, and that smile was meant for her, she knew he loved her in his own way. And she knew she loved that man.

They'd been in the water well over an hour, which was more than Sandra could ever remember, when her dad gave her a signal that he was going down one more time. Thumbs up from both of them, and they'd call it a day. First Sandra thought it was her imagination – a sharp tug from the floats that were attached to her by a length of heavy fishing line. Then it happened again, and she was sure it was her father playing a trick on her. She'd been captivated by a small manta ray she could see half-buried on the bottom of the bay. This time she turned to see if her dad was going to grab her leg in jest when she saw the giant thing heading for the fish on the float for a third time. She had seen "Finding Nemo" not long before on television, and was certain she was seeing the monster fish from the ocean depths with the little light that revealed nothing but a giant mouth full of razor-sharp teeth. This one didn't have a light dangling in front of it, but she saw the rows of teeth as it ripped two of the fish off of the line, not fifteen feet from where her fins were.

She had let go of the line like it was on fire, and gulped a gallon of water into her snorkel as she tried to put as much space between herself and "Jaws" as possible. When she spotted her dad coming up with two good-sized fish, she tried to call his name, but the only thing that came out was a loud "Owwwwhh!!!" like something you might hear if a cat got thrown into a barrel of cold water. She didn't know what she was saying, but she was screaming it at the top of her lungs. Her dad heard something, and picked up his pace until he was close enough to make out the frantic features of her face.

When he reached the surface, she was able to grab her facemask and fling it backward and tell him that a sea monster was after them and they needed to get out of the water, not now, but RIGHT now.

Her father had responded by taking another breath and sinking down in the water to get a look at what was happening. That's when he came face-to-teeth with the most ferocious fish in the ocean, a giant barracuda. It had torn the last of the fish from the float line, and had smelled the blood from the two remaining ones in Ergeny's left hand. Sandra had managed to get her mask on again and watched as her father stared down the beast, held out the two fish at arm's length, and as the barracuda made a motion toward them, he let them drop from his grasp. He had torn the gills free before surfacing, so that they wouldn't float on their own, and the two fish began a slow descent, like two leaves falling from a tree in a light breeze. The barracuda knew a gift when he saw one, and circled down toward the first fish. While he went after the appetizer, Ergeny calmly cocked the rubber ropes of his spear gun, and floated on the surface, both hands on the gun to keep it as steady as possible. When the barracuda was directly below him and preparing to grab the second fish, he pulled the trigger and the spear pierced the back of the monster's skull.

Sandra would have nightmares for weeks about the way the beast that was twice her weight came up and after her father, blood rushing from the wounds on the top and bottom of its head. He had used his empty spear gun as a bat to swat it away, losing his grip on the gun and getting a sampling of the sharpness of the teeth as it scraped against his right forearm. Like a Hollywood stunt double, Ergeny had made a half-twist in the water, and got one hand on each side of the spear that protruded evenly from both sides of its head and held on for his life while the barracuda wanted nothing more than to take him with it to the grave. The teeth chomped as it thrashed with all of its remaining strength to get close enough to sink its jaws into the enemy. Ergeny had to have known if he couldn't hold on, it might have enough strength left to kill both him and his daughter, so he kept his arms locked straight and stared into the eyes of the beast that would either die or kill him. He hadn't filled his lungs with air in time, though, and would eventually need to let go and surface.

Sandra watched in terror, and realized after what seemed like infinity that she had been counting since her father had gone into mortal combat with the monster. A hundred seconds had passed, and she was sure that the monster was getting stronger instead of weaker. She was certain she was watching her father's last moments alive.

The line was still attached to the gun that had gone down when Ergeny lost his grip on it, and it now bounced along the bottom of the bay as the stand-off continued above. Sandra saw the fish make a funny half-twist in the water and stop dead, still thrashing. She watched her father let go of the spear, and thought he was giving up. That's when she saw that the gun had acted as an anchor, and had become trapped between two heavy rocks.

Unbelievably, she saw that amazing smile on her father's face as he raced up for a breath of oxygen. Instead of going back down, though, he floated over next to her, like a protective father, and pointed with her as they watched the life wane from the biggest fish Sandra had ever seen.

When he was sure it was dead, he calmly dove down and yanked the gun from the rocks and used it as a tow rope to pull the giant beast to the shore. All they had as transportation was one bicycle with a rack on the back where Sandra had carried the spear gun on their way to the bay, some ten kilometers from Trinidad. When he tried to lift it onto the rack, the head rested on the ground on one side while the tail dragged on the opposite side. He tried tying the head to the handlebars and the tail to the rack, but the weight of the middle kept dragging him down. Sandra wanted so badly to take a picture of her father with the giant fish, but she had never had a camera of her own. A honk from the highway leading to the "Trinidad del Mar" hotel saved Ergeny from having to cut the beast into chunks to get it home. One of the drivers from the hotel had spotted them in their struggle, and parked the panel van as near to them as possible. It turned out to be a friend of her Uncle Felix, and everybody knew Ergeny. He supplied most of the lobster the tourists loved so much in the hotel. The driver helped Ergeny maneuver the barracuda into the van, along with the bicycle, and then held the front door open for Sandra.

The monster fish barely fit in the cargo area of the small van. The two men discussed if either had ever seen a bigger one, and they decided this was the grandfather of all barracudas that had ever graced the waters of Casilda. The driver suggested it would be a perfect tourist attraction at the hotel, and he could help Ergeny to get paid at least a hundred dollars for it.

Sandra remembered how he had given her the final decision – sell it or eat it. Given the fact she was still shaking from the experience, she decided she had seen all she wanted of this animal. "Take the hundred dollars," she had told him. "You can buy a lot of fish for a hundred dollars."

They turned the van back toward the hotel and the driver called four kitchen staffers to haul it into the hotel. The manager was more than happy to oblige with the purchase, since there was already a crowd of tourists snapping pictures and trying to get their hands on it.

Sandra asked if somebody could take a picture of her and her father with the fish, even if she never saw a copy of it. They found a place to pose with it, and dozens of cameras recorded the moment. Sandra asked the manager to let her know if he ever received a copy from any of them.

Ergeny helped get it into the kitchen, and they refused the offer of a lift into Trinidad. He preferred to spend the hour and a half peddling back into the city with his daughter. He had to have been completely exhausted, if Sandra felt as drained as she did, but he never complained once on the ride home. His muscular legs kept a steady rhythm past the Costa Sur, past the Grille restaurant at the fork in the road that led to La Boca to the left or Trinidad to the right.

They didn't speak on the trip home, but Sandra knew they had shared something extra-special that no one could ever take away from them.

Arriving at her house, after dark, Sandra saw her mother waiting in the doorway with an annoyed look on her face. "All that time and no fish for your dinner? Didn't you catch anything?" She could see her mother was annoyed as usual with her ex.

"Caught one, but it got away," was his only reply. That smile again, and he flipped her a thumbs up, and kissed her on the cheek. He stuffed something into her pocket as he kissed her, and rode away with the same steady rhythm.

"Now I have to invent something to make for dinner. I was counting on a few fresh fish. Your father never changes. I suppose he stopped for a beer and never even got wet."

Sandra slipped past her mother while she continued her commentary about her father and all of his faults. She was anxious to see what he had stuffed into her pocket, but wanted to be alone. She went into the bathroom and closed the door behind her. It was the only room in the house with a lock. She felt herself smiling for no good reason as she reached into her pocket and felt the paper. There was something inside the folded paper, too. She sat on the edge of the seat-less toilet, and unfolded the surprise carefully. Inside was a hundred dollar bill, four of the biggest fangs she had ever seen, and a few words scrawled on the paper. "Buy that washing machine your mother's always talking about. I got my hundred dollars' worth spending a day with my beautiful daughter".

When he'd invited her to fish with him again a few months later, he wasn't surprised when Sandra politely refused. Fishing wasn't for her. She was glad to see he sported the neck chain she'd had made from three of the teeth. A friend in the Candonga had made it for her. The fourth tooth was safely locked away in her treasure box.

Strangely, her fantasies of a reunion between her father and mother went away after that afternoon in the bay. She knew he was a womanizing jerk, and had never been much of a father to her, let alone Ergeny, whom he seemed to loathe for some reason, and Fidel hadn't even had a year in the same house as their father. Who knew how long little Edith would get with him before he moved onto number five? He was who he was. Sandra thought about that old saying, 'you don't get to choose your family', and she knew even if she had known how brief her time with him was going to be, she would have chosen him for her father, anyway.

Nearly six months later, long after she'd stopped expecting it, the driver from the Trinidad del Mar pulled up to the house in the same little panel van, and knocked on the door.

Sandra answered with a questioning look on her face. "Hey, how are you? You're the friend of my Uncle Felix that helped us with the fish that day."

"Thought you'd want this right away. It came from Germany this afternoon."

He pulled the small box from the passenger seat of the van. Sandra noticed it had been opened.

"It was addressed to the manager, so he opened it. There were three – one was for him, the note said."

Sandra unwrapped the framed pictures – they had been professionally developed and framed with oak – you could see Sandra struggled to hold up the back half of the barracuda, but Ergeny displayed his patented white smile. What Sandra noticed right away was her father's smile was directed at her, not the camera and not the fish.

She couldn't wait to get his copy to him, so she grabbed the old Russian tank, as she called it, and took a running start so as not to strip the gears any more than they already were, and headed to the Barranca, where her father lived with the wife nearly her age, and little Edith.

When she pulled up outside the house, she could hear her father's wife, Theresa, screaming at him because he had come home drunk again, and who was the little slut he'd been dancing with... probably the exact words he'd heard at least three times before. She heard Edith crying, and decided this wasn't the time to interrupt. She was about to climb on the tank again to go home when she heard a voice calling to her. She raised her finger to her lips to shhh him from calling again. It was a school friend from junior high who lived a block from her father.

She decided to ask Julio Cesar to deliver the picture once the action had died down. He just shook his head. It turned out the girl Ergeny had been caught with at the Cave nightclub was his half-sister on his father's side. She was barely eighteen, and Ergeny was pushing forty-five.

Sandra laughed out loud. Julio Cesar looked at her, wondering what was funny about the situation.

"Sorry about that, Julio; it's just I read a magazine article recently about the six degrees of separation, and it just occurred to me if my father married your sister, you'd be my uncle." They both laughed. Sandra slid the picture out of the paper wrapping, and showed it to Julio Cesar.

"I've been hearing about this for months," exclaimed Julio. "Everybody's been saying your father was making it up."

Sandra marveled again at the smile on her father's face, looking over at her in the picture. She thought about how much her mother loved the washing machine she had bought the next day. She knew there was no washing machine where Ergeny lived here in the Barranca. That hundred dollars would have gone a long way to help with little Edith. On the other hand, she'd slept with him, knowing he was still married to Fidel's mother. She wasn't any innocent victim.

She gave Julio Cesar a hug and a kiss on the cheek, and left him the picture to deliver to her father once there was a lull in the battle, and walked her bike back to the paved street. There were so many potholes in the cobblestone streets here that even walking was difficult. She thought about her father, and how one day soon he would probably be saying good-bye to wife and child number four, and another little girl would grow up with step-fathers who stared at her just a little too long. Maybe one day, when she was older, little Edith would be invited to spend the afternoon fishing with her father.

She hoped so.

When she got home, Sandra flipped open her magazine to the Kevin Bacon story. In the picture, he flashed a broad smile.

"You got nothin' on my old man," she said to the picture. Her barracuda tooth felt cool and smooth between her thumb and fingers.

E R G E N Y
J R

The Gold Watch

His name should have been better... that was Ergeny's one flaw. Oh, and he should have been ten feet tall, too. Heroes and legends were always tall. By the time he was a seventeen-year-old kid, he already owned his own home, and had a baby on the way with his twenty-two-year-old wife. He was a shining star by then, though. Leading men – the Brad Pitts, the Tom Cruises, the Leonardo DiCaprios – they all had the package, and it always included a perfect smile and to-die-for eyes. Ergeny had a better smile than Cruise, better eyes than Pitt, and a better body than DiCaprio. He had the charm and charisma that drew people to him and made them want to lift him up to be president of the free world.

Okay, that was one other flaw Ergeny had. He didn't live in the free world. He lived in a five hundred year old colonial city on the Caribbean island of Cuba called Trinidad.

In Latin America, it's an old custom that a son be given his father's first name – usually the first son. In this culture, children have two last names – the first sir name of their father, and the first sir name of their mother. So to cement the pride of the family in their son, they give him the same given name as their father.

Ergeny grew up in a loving home, raised by his doting mother, Lillet, who, unfortunately found solace in bottles of rum when her husband was off doing his thing. His father, also Ergeny, left her for a younger woman before the third birthday celebration. Ergeny Senior was a gifted diver, and lobster was a treasured commodity in the tightly-controlled economy. There would always be a market for lobster and other fresh seafood, be it in the all-inclusive hotels or with the lucky few who had a supply of the cherished green-backs from a Miami connection. More often than not, his customers were the very people who preached to the masses about equality and sacrifice for the revolution – the party officials and military elite who drank fine wine and the actual Havana Club rum, not the swill that they sold on the street to the "regular" Cubans. That stuff tasted suspiciously like the liquid that ran the Russian tractors in the sugar cane fields.

One of the most important by-products of being a diver is the physique it provides. Being able to hold your breath for more than four minutes at a time naturally expands the lungs, little by little, until the chest cavity is unusually large, and the muscles that are formed by dozens of hours a day in the water are pronounced – arms, legs, a barrel chest, and a wash-board stomach without ever doing a single sit-up. Add to that a perfect bronze tan, and unusually shiny eyes from hours of exposure to salt, and I'm sure you're starting to get the picture and can understand why divers don't make for good husbands and fathers in Cuba.

That Ergeny would follow his absent father into the ocean was no surprise to anyone. There were many who thought it was cute or romantic that he would choose the same path as his estranged dad, but they didn't really get it. He didn't do it out of love or respect – he did it to prove he could do anything better than the sperm-donor who denied to anyone who asked that he was the father.

Half a day's walk from Trinidad there is a beautiful waterfall that feeds a deep river. It's too far from the paved roads to be a tourist attraction, or the government would have surely denied access to Cubans. The only foreigners to visit the swimming mecca were those whose Cuban friends or family convinced it was worth nearly dying of exposure to reach. The falls were almost twenty meters in height, and the volume of water that fell was strong enough to have carved a crater ten meters in depth and five in diameter. Cuban teenagers would pack a lunch and leave home early in the morning, before the mid-day sun could bake them, and make a day out of it, not returning home until the sun was on its way down, but still early enough that they could make out the hand-and foot-holds they needed to climb up and out of the sanctuary.

So the legend goes somebody's rich cousin from the U.S. made the trip to the falls and tried to climb up and under the cascade. He caught his gold watch on a sharp rock and the strap broke. It plunged into the water at its deepest point, and everyone there watched the American dive in over and over again, but he never came close to reaching the bottom. He apparently wasn't supposed to have been wearing the watch, which was some family heirloom, and feared for his hide when he had to tell his parents he'd lost it. When he finally conceded he wasn't ever going to get it, he made it known to the bathers there he'd pay two hundred dollars to anyone who returned the watch to him. Two hundred dollars, in 2001, was the equivalent in Cuban pesos to the annual salary of a doctor in Cuba, so there were a few divers that day who risked cutting themselves on the rocks on their way home after the sun went down, doing their best to challenge their own lungs to find the bottom. None came close.

There was an old joke where a husband said to his loving wife, "These past ten years with you have felt like five minutes." She smiles and gives him an affectionate squeeze, when he adds, "But five minutes under water." It cracks people up every time – mostly the men.

Ergeny was the only person around who could actually say that to his wife and not be making a joke. He had expanded his lungs over his already ten-plus years of free diving to the point that holding his breath for five minutes was as normal to him as a carpenter driving a four inch spike in two hits. It was just part of what he did.

Somebody who knew Ergeny let him know about the watch and the offer, and the very next morning, with his lunch packed, he made his way to the waterfall. Trinidad is a city, but with a small-town atmosphere, and rumors and gossip were rampant. A two-hundred dollar bounty for a watch had already rippled up and down every cobble-stone street in the museum city. Old ladies on stoops spoke about it, and older men speculated that in their day they could have gotten it. Everyone thought about what they would or could do with two hundred dollars. For most of them, a month's salary was in the neighborhood of $7.00 U.S. Basic necessities were for the most part covered by the quota book – a few kilos of rice, beans, sugar, salt, and enough coffee for a taste every day. So when people saw Ergeny with a bag lunch in his hand, those who had no other pressing business that day, and most didn't, quickly filled their own pack and headed toward the falls.

To get to the site, two trails converged half a mile from the river – one fork led to the east side of the city and the other more to the west. As mentioned earlier, word travelled fast around the small city of the fabulous reward for retrieving the gold watch from the depths. What turned things into a real event was that the news had been delivered to both Ergenys – father and son – the two best divers in Trinidad. Two separate groups of fans followed their respective Ergeny and they merged almost simultaneously where the two trails met. Since Ergeny Senior didn't recognize Ergeny Junior as his child, he ignored the teenager and continued. People commented to their friends at the irony, considering they were almost perfect copies. Some snickered at the indifference, and others shook their heads in disgust. There was a definite age difference between the two groups, and almost immediately there were chides thrown between them. Someone suggested betting on who would come up with the watch, and things got downright exciting. Youth versus experience. Father versus son.

When they arrived at the swimming hole, no one entered the water. Everyone found a comfortable vantage point, and from nowhere bottles of the diesel-like rum started making their rounds in the groups. There was a party-like atmosphere, and someone had brought a portable radio with them that played some awful-sounding music, but it was music all the same. Beautiful young women showed off their tanned bodies as they preened on large flat rocks, while boys who were brave in their groups made cat-calls at them.

When Ergeny Senior pulled out a set of diving fins and a mask, there were audible cheers from his supporters and calls of foul from the younger side. While the older diver slipped on his equipment, preparing to be first in the water, Ergeny Junior calmly chewed on his sandwich and sliced an avocado that he'd packed with his trusty utility knife he never went anywhere without. People tried to encourage him to hurry, not to let his father beat him to the prize. He just chewed and smiled and chatted quietly with the people closest to him. Somebody offered him a bottle of rum, but he thanked them and waved it off.

Senior turned his back to the falls and let himself fall into the cold water, to the cheers of his supporters. The young side turned their heads in unison to see the reaction from their prospect. They were disappointed. Instead of hurrying down to the water, Ergeny Junior finished his lunch, folded the plastic bag and methodically tucked it into his pocket. There was a rumble of nervous energy from his father's supporters, as he had been under water for more than a minute already.

Hearts stopped collectively as they saw his shape appearing from the depths, and everyone searched his hands for the treasure as he surfaced. He caught sight of someone he knew, and shook his head. He mouthed that it was too dark – he couldn't see anything. He relaxed a few minutes, and then disappeared once again. Eyes once again flew to Junior, who seemed as indifferent as ever. He seemed to be just another spectator in the crowd, showing no intention to get wet. He glanced over his shoulder occasionally, and sipped on his bottle of ice water.

Senior surfaced a half dozen times, always with the same frustration of not being able to see anything. The crowd got less interested with each failed attempt, and got more interested in the baseball game being broadcast over the little radio. When he came up with the bottom of a bikini, there was a roar of laughter from both sides.

After what was at least an hour from Senior's first dive, Junior slipped off his walking shorts, showing off the form-fitting Lycra bicycle shorts some tourist had traded for a bag of river prawns. There were some oohs and ahhs and giggles from the younger girls, but when he stood up and peeled off his shirt, young girls and old girls let out involuntary sounds that probably echoed into the depths where his father continued to blindly flail about, hoping for the watch to jump into his hands.

Junior glanced once again over his shoulder to where the sun was just then peeking over the tree line and erasing the shadows that covered the rocks and river bank. He took that as his signal and started to move. People got excited again, but only briefly, because instead of making his way down to the river's edge, Junior started back up the trail. Some speculated he'd given up, since he hadn't brought fins or a mask, and even with those, his father hadn't managed to find the watch. People from the father's camp made suggestions the other side pay up on the bet because the younger one had given up. There were some harsh words and even some pushing and shoving, until someone pointed out Junior had abandoned the trail out of the valley and had instead started toward the upper ledge where the falls originated. He was crazy, they all decided. The walls of the gorge were glass-smooth and ninety degrees to the river. There was no place to hold on to climb down from there.

Women began to call out to him to be careful, not to get too close to the edge. A little girl who had come with her parents started to cry when she saw how small Ergeny looked so far up from the river bank. Even so far away, the smile was still evident on the young man's face, and he looked positively God-like, standing on that ledge in all his glory. Adults speculated about what would happen if he should fall from that height, and some even shaded their children's eyes so they wouldn't witness what would surely cause nightmares for months.

Senior had had enough of this game, and when he surfaced the next time, he slid out of the water and pulled off his mask and fins, rolling his eyes at the futility. Someone got his attention and pointed up to where his younger self was perched. He shook his head, and there was a flicker of concern he quickly tried to cover by turning his back and calling for the nearest bottle of rum. He took a long pull on the bottle, and sighed at the failed attempt to be a hero. He'd already spent and re-spent the two hundred dollars in his mind a dozen times. Oh well, he thought… nobody was going to get it if he hadn't found it in more than ten attempts.

It was at that very moment the sun escaped its shackles and a warmth spread over the river bank, and the surface of the water changed colors from opaque to sparkling clear. Senior was taking another long drink of rum when he saw the flicker of sunlight in the depths of the water. He closed his eyes and shook his head and reached back for his fins and mask. As he struggled to pull his left fin on, he heard the collective gasp from the crowd, and looked up just in time to see the most beautiful sight – his son flying through the air in a perfect swan dive. There was time for women and girls to scream and men to swear while Junior descended in slow motion, waiting until the last possible instant to tuck his head, with the smile still visible, between his outstretched arms to plummet into the water like a javelin, straight to the bottom.

His father was still pulling on his mask when a fist punched out of the water, just beside the spray of the falls, and the cheer that followed when they saw the gold watch in his open hand was like the winning goal of the world cup, won by the home team in the last seconds of the game. Both sides screamed their approval – everyone felt like they were part of the victory.

Junior made his way to the edge, and walked past his father to hand the watch to a pal who extended his hand to help him over the slippery rocks. People who didn't know him wanted to touch him. He was a real live hero, in a place where there was little to cheer about.

That would have been enough for most people in Cuba. Heck, for most people anywhere. Ergeny wasn't most people, though. He shook all of the hands offered to him, even kissed a beautiful young girl on the lips, raising another cheer from the crowd, but instead of stopping to dry himself off and get dressed, he made his way back up to the cliff again. Half of the crowd had already started making their way to the trail out of the valley and had to stop and find another place to watch from. What did this guy want to go and risk his life again for? He already had the watch, and he could build a house from the two hundred dollars it would fetch.

This time he didn't waste any precious seconds. He wanted to use the window of sunlight as quickly as he could, and before his father could finish pulling off his fins for the second time, he launched himself into the air again, plunging once more into the water with barely a splash. He would have received a ten from the Russian judge at the Olympics for that one. This time, though, something was different. This time he didn't resurface within thirty seconds like the previous dive. For the average person, two minutes under water is a very long time, and the crowd began to murmur after what seemed to be an eternity. There were no longer any ripples on the surface from his entry, and the comments turned from mild concern to serious doubt to outright panic. By the time three minutes had passed, people started to call for help. A couple of Junior's friends pulled off their outer clothes and dove into the water, trying to make their way into the depths. Both came up empty-handed and someone screamed at Senior to do something. By the time he'd once again pulled his fins on and grabbed for his mask, four minutes had passed and still no sign of Junior.

Now more spectators jumped into the water, desperate to try to do something, knowing there was little they could do. Senior plunged in again, turning himself vertical to go as deep as he could as quickly as possible. Women and children cried as they scoured the surface for signs of life from their new hero. The question on everyone's lips was 'why – why did he dive in again after he had the prize already?'

Somebody could be heard to say five minutes had passed, and people buried their heads in their hands. Such a waste. Such a tragedy, after a triumph so big.

Amid the anguish and crying, a young boy jumped and pointed. "There! Behind the falls!"

No one paid much attention, assuming it was one of the would-be rescuers. The mist from the falls was too thick to make out any features, but there definitely was someone back there. Just as he had appeared, he disappeared again, and people began to think they had just imagined it. Senior surfaced with a distraught look on his face – he had found nothing on the bottom.

Then from beside the falls a head popped back up to the surface and this time there was no denying that it was Junior. Some were afraid that it was his lifeless body floating up from the depths, until he rolled onto his back and flashed his million-dollar grin. He thrust his right hand into the air once again, and pumped his fist three times in victory. One of the swimmers who'd jumped in was close enough to see what he had in his hand.

"It's the pin from the watch band!"

And THAT'S when the legend was born.

A couple of days later, when Ergeny Senior stepped out of his house to head out for a day of diving, he found a small brown box hanging from the door handle. Inside, with no note, was the gold watch, including the strap that had been repaired with the tiny pin.

FIDEL

The Young Man and the River

There was something twisted in the naming of sons in the family, he had been sure of it. What had his parents been thinking? Who named their son Fidel? He'd been teased his entire life – "Where's your beard, Fidel?", "Let's play revolution, Commandant." He knew he had been named after his grandfather's brother, on his mother's side, so he couldn't really blame his father, although it was more fun to blame him.

Thanks to that name he'd grown up something of a loner. He saw his dad around town, with the new baby girl he had with his fourth wife. Fidel's mother had been the third, and had gotten pregnant while he was still with number two. Shouldn't have expected anything different – he was too handsome and had too much spare money not to take advantage of every skirt that passed by him. He was a lobster diver, and lobster divers worked three days a week for the government, filling the quotas of the all-inclusive hotels that lined the beach on the Ancon Peninsula, a few short miles from Trinidad, one of the Unesco World Heritage sites. The good news was he had two half-sisters and a half-brother. His father didn't seem to like to have two kids with any one woman.

Fidel couldn't help but be drawn to the ocean. His mother told him he had salt water in his veins. At twelve, he could already hold his breath for nearly four minutes. People said his old man could stay under for more than five, but he figured it was an exaggeration.

If he ever passed close to his father at the market, he'd hear him telling the baby she had a big brother who would look out for her. That made him feel strange. His dad didn't ever talk directly to Fidel, but he seemed happy to talk *about* him when he knew he was within earshot. He would always make a big show about carrying the heaviest sacks of food from the farmer's market, to prove to everyone around he had money to burn. None of the food was ever dropped off for Fidel's mother, though. He would ride right past their house with his mountain bike weighed down so much that the tires bulged, and would look right at them.

Fidel's mother, Maria, crocheted clothing out of the cotton string they used for tying the bundles of tobacco. She paid a fee to have a tiny little stall in the tourist market so the "Yumas", as they were called behind their backs, had something to spend their money on when they came to Trinidad on the tour buses. His half-sister, Sandra, also had a stall, not far from his mother's. Fidel's mom was the prettiest in the whole market, and sold enough vests and bags to keep them fed and dry. He had a uniform for school that was always perfectly clean and ironed, shoes and clothes to play, and one pair of pants and a long-sleeved shirt for the rare times that his mother found an extra dollar that wasn't for the rent of her stall. Fidel dreamed of having their own television, a color one like the Aguila's down the street. They were mean, and closed the shutters and the door to the street whenever they watched it, so the kids from the block didn't converge on their stoop to watch cartoons or the baseball game. He knew his dad had a color television already, and he sometimes imagined at night that his father would knock on the door and surprise them with one.

Fidel had only asked his mother once why she didn't tell his father to give them money or food. She had yelled at him louder than ever, and then he'd heard her crying in the bathroom later. That was the night Fidel had decided it was time for him to start contributing to the family coffers. But what could he do? He couldn't crochet, and there were no jobs for kids in Cuba.

It was his father who had provided him the answer... not because Fidel had asked him for advice and he had stopped in the market to pat him on the head, and had suggested he go and live with him in the new house he was going to build in La Boca, with the view of the beach. It was only because he'd seen his father pass by early the following morning with his fins and snorkel and mask, on his way to pay for the new refrigerator they needed for their other house and their new baby.

When his mother left for the market the following Saturday morning, Fidel packed a lunch of a chunk of bread and an avocado and tomato that he'd squirrelled away. He couldn't walk to the ocean to dive for lobsters – it was ten kilometers, and he had no dive suit or fins. He had another destination, only half a mile from the entrance to Trinidad. His cousin Miguel Enrique, who was five years older, was his father's sister's oldest, and he told Fidel stories about the sacks of fresh-water shrimp, or prawns, that his father used to bring home for family feasts. Fidel knew that he could sell them with no problem – the Aguila's always had money for luxuries.

It was a half hour's walk to the monument to Trinidad at the entrance to the city from Cienfuegos, an hour to the east, and the hill was long and steep leading down to the curve where the Guaurabo River wound slowly toward the ocean at La Boca. He stopped in the shade of the monument and ate half of his bread, slicing the avocado and tomato onto it with the kitchen knife he'd slipped out of the drawer after his mother had washed it carefully. They only had the one sharp knife, so Fidel knew he needed to take good care of it. Some tourists stopped to take pictures at the monument, and Fidel took that as his cue to move along. He didn't know what to say to them – he didn't think they'd understand the basic words he'd been learning in school, and didn't feel like being laughed at. Somebody would surely ask his name, and he didn't know how to just lie and say it was Julio or Alexander or any other normal name. "Where's your friend, Che?" one of them would inevitably ask, chuckling to his buddies.

The biggest problem Fidel faced now was the fact that he knew from what Miguel Enrique had told him – in order to get the prawns he had to let them bite his hand that he shoved into the dark caves in the rocks – and he couldn't just yank his hand out when something touched it. He knew those things clamped on like crazy when they did. You had to be brave. Fidel knew he was a good swimmer, and staying underwater long enough wasn't going to be his problem. He just wasn't brave. He was still scared of the dark – he slept with a light on in the kitchen.

As he approached the bridge over the river, where he planned to do his hunting, Fidel tried pinching his own hands and fingers to acclimatize them, so to speak. Once he felt like the pinches didn't bother him, he tried biting himself. He still had his right hand clenched firmly in his mouth when he rounded the edge of the bridge and surprised a teen-aged couple who were there kissing. He almost drew blood, yanking his hand out of his teeth so quickly. The couple were equally surprised, and decided to find a better place now that this one had been discovered.

While he walked, it was his habit to play out childish fantasies in his head. Most of these involved candy and flowers being delivered to their house by his father, who swept his mother off her feet and they became a family again. His mother would make yellow rice with big chunks of pork in it, and there would be ice cream for dessert. Fidel's hand absently reached into his pocket where he kept the flat stone. Others sometimes speculated as to the sentimental value it must have had, since he never went anywhere without it. The truth was, the ancient Russian bike his mother took him to school and to his grandparents' house on had a twisted rear sprocket, and would invariably lock up at least once every trip. As the man of the house, he took the responsibility to find a rock to beat the chain back into place so they could continue their journey. Finally, he got tired of having to rummage around looking for a suitable rock, so he decided to carry his "tool kit" with him, and when he found a rock that didn't tear holes in his pockets or chafe his leg, he hung onto it. He called it his David and Goliath stone, because it was round and smooth like he'd imagined David's had been. He almost used it once on one of the men who made suggestive remarks to his mother. One of them offered to trade his own mother for Fidel's. He had scowled his best scowl and replied, "Sure, yours is old and wrinkled and mine is super sexy!" His mother had laughed all the way to her sister's house that night.

Now he was at the river's edge, and found a space where he could keep his clothes dry and out of the sun. He had his swimming trunks on under his slacks, and carefully unwrapped the set of goggles some tourist had tossed out in the trash beside the Ancon Hotel. Fidel had fished them out and carefully cleaned them and fixed the part that had broken, where the strap attached to it. The goggles made it so much easier to see underwater.

He stuck a toe into the river's edge and yanked it out just as quickly. The water felt like he might be able to skate on it instead of swim in it. The ocean was so much warmer than the rivers that fed into it. Fidel saw the shadow from the bridge overhead, and knew he'd already wasted more time than he could afford. His mother would be home by four from the market, and she was a worrier.

There was no going back empty-handed now. He did what he always did when he had to shower at home with cold water – he counted to three, and closed his eyes and jumped. The cold water assaulted him from every direction, but Fidel loved water. His mother always told him he must have been a fish in a previous life, because once in the water, he never wanted to get out.

Once the initial shock had worn off, he opened his eyes and waited until the water cleared and he could see something around him. The water was crystal clear once the silt had settled from his jumping in. He still had the goggles in his hand, and as he broke the surface of the river to catch his breath, he spit into each lens and rubbed his finger around in them. Rolling onto his back, he lounged on the surface while he slipped them on and carefully adjusted the straps. He twisted himself until he was face-down, and was pleased to see the bottom of the river without any trouble.

Now he heard the lessons of his cousin Miguel Enrique again in his head, but this time he exchanged his cousin's image for that of his father, as though it was really his father guiding him as to how to catch the elusive prawns. "You have to look for anything that can act as a cave," his father explained, full of patience and pride. "Watch for overhanging rocks. They love the shade."

Fidel floated lazily on the surface, scanning the river bottom for signs of movement in the rocks.

The river was about ten feet deep, here under the bridge, and about thirty feet across. Under the concrete cover there wasn't enough sunlight for the weeds to grow, so the rocks were more exposed. That was why Miguel Enrique had told him to try there first. At first it seemed he had been mistaken, because for the first few minutes, he could see nothing that looked even remotely like a cave. That was because he was looking for a cave like the ones in the cartoons he had seen, peeking through open doorways at neighbors' television sets, until their cross looks sent him packing. He loved the coyote and roadrunner, and there were always caves and tunnels.

There: he knew he had seen a movement off to his left – something had definitely emerged from under a big rock and disappeared just as quickly. He fixed his gaze there and tried to keep himself as still as possible. He sang the national anthem to himself; that was his concentration trick. He would try to sing it from start to finish as many times as possible, and not think about how much he wanted to take a breath.

This time was no mistake – there was something under that rock, and he was sure he saw a claw. He felt his heart-rate soar in his chest. Not because he had seen the prey, but because he knew he wasn't ready for the pain he was going to suffer in order to get it. He made a mental note of exactly where it was, so when he went up to take a few breaths and prepare himself, he wouldn't have to spend time finding it again.

He pushed the thoughts of the pain out of his head, replacing them with the smile on his mother's face when he handed her the money he would get for the prawns. He thought about the washing machine she so badly needed, and the color television and the new bicycle with gears. He didn't know why, but he imagined his father riding beside her with him on the rack behind him. They were headed for the beach...

He heard his father's voice again, reminding him that when the prawn clamped onto his finger, he had to leave it there until he got it out of the water. If he tried to yank it off, he would tear the skin of his finger open because the claws were like sharp knives.

He drew in a deep breath and with the rock in his sights, he rolled in the water to begin his descent, trying to keep his movements as calm as he could. This was really happening! He was going to catch his first freshwater prawn. His father would be so proud of him. He was on the riverbed, now, and as his cousin had told him, he grabbed a couple of heavy stones to help him maintain himself on the bottom. He held the biggest one with his left hand and let go of the one in his right. He couldn't let himself wait or he would talk himself out of it – he thrust his hand in, but too fast, and felt the giant shrimp-like creature scurry out of reach. He let half of his breath go at that instant, and remembered he couldn't do anything quickly. It had to be slow and deliberate, and the prawn had to feel threatened enough to turn and fight.

He debated returning to the surface for a fresh breath, but decided he still had well over a minute left, and he was already at the right rock. He started to sing the Cuban anthem in his head. "Al combate corred bayameses..." He sang it every morning before classes, and still wasn't completely sure what some of the words meant. His favorite part was where they sang that dying for their country was to live. "Al morir por la Patria es vivir." He was just at that phrase when he slid his hand under the rock, slowly this time. After that line in the anthem came a big three beat "dum dum dum" of the drums, and it was on the second "dum" that Fidel felt what seemed like a thousand volt electric shock.

He immediately regretted his decision not to have gone up for more air, because his underwater scream took care of everything else left in his lungs. He bolted for the surface, swallowing a mouthful of water and coughed and sputtered and gyrated his way to the edge of the river where he threw himself onto the bank, ignoring the sharpness of the rocks. He wondered how anything could be so painful, and decided then and there that prawn diving was for people much crazier than he was.

Just as he was about to examine the damage to his finger, he realized there was still a creature attached to him. It looked more like the alien from the Saturday night movies than anything anyone would want to eat. His first reaction was to get it off of him as fast as he could, which of course was exactly the opposite of the advice he'd received from his cousin/father. Lessons are learned the hard way, though, and Fidel learned the hard way what happened when skin and muscle battle with the razor-sharp claws from a crustacean. The tiny trickle of blood that had been seeping from the edges of the point where the prawn clung to him became a gushing flesh wound that turned the water red around him as he threw the beast onto the rocks beside him. He realized at that instant the pain from the prawn clamping down on his finger wasn't so bad after all.

This pain – that was bad.

He heard the clop clop clop of hooves and tires above him, which could only come from a carreton, the two-wheeled carts that were used as local transport for everything from ice from the factory outside of the city to gravel for construction projects to full-blown home relocation. With the divorce rate as high as it was in Trinidad, being a carretonero was a pretty good job. Fidel listened to the sound as it faded from earshot, while his cousin's rule that men don't cry from pain echoed in his mind. They could cry when they were sad, like when his great grandmother passed a few months earlier from the cancer in her bones. They could cry when they were really happy, like Uncle Felix had when Sancti Spiritus finally won the baseball championship. Of course he'd been so drunk that day he'd thrown up when he coughed, and his cousin Jose Antonio had to carry him to bed.

Fidel was so busy not crying from the pain he almost didn't see the monster wiggling and twitching its way back to the water's edge. Two or three more gyrations of its tail and tentacles and it would have had quite a story to tell its grandchildren, or grand-prawns, as it were. Grabbing a tree branch within reach, Fidel swatted it back onto the dry grass a few yards up the bank. He wasn't going near that monster with any part of himself again, that was certain. He was sure he could see a smile on its alien-like face, like on that movie he'd watched one Saturday night before his mother made him turn it off and go to bed. He hadn't slept much that night.

He felt like he was only bending the rule a little bit, in case he needed to justify himself to Miguel Enrique, because he decided he would just cry a little bit now, but because he was so happy to have caught his first prawn, and two dollars was enough to make any man cry in Cuba!

He cried for a minute, letting the nervous energy of what had happened seep out of his system, while he watched the creature's gyrations diminish as the air drowned it. He wondered if it felt any pain, if dying from breathing air was anything like drowning in water. He didn't feel a lot of pity, seeing a piece of his finger skin still attached to the claw.

The crying turned into laughter. Uncontrollable. Kicking his feet laughter. Screaming out loud. When he finally stopped laughing, Fidel looked around to make sure no one had witnessed his madness. There was only a skinny horse and some buzzards in sight.

Buzzards. Dead animals. Sharp teeth and talons that could tear open a cow. Might be a good idea to cover up the prawn that could be swept away in a second by one of those hideous bald bas-. Even to himself Fidel stopped short of swearing. His mother didn't allow any foul language, and his internal reprimand kicked in. He remembered the plastic bag in his backpack and quickly manipulated the prawn into it with the stick, even though it wasn't moving anymore. Better safe than sorry. He tore off a strip of plastic about two inches wide and made several wraps around his finger. He'd gotten a quick glimpse as he let go with his free hand, and started working on a good lie to tell his mother. He was content with the first aid job as he slipped the free end between the two fingers and squeezed them together to hold it in place.

He was proud of his Cuban heritage at that moment. Every self-respecting Cuban carried a plastic bag in his pocket whenever he left the house. Food was priority one for every man, woman and child on the island, and there was nothing more important than having some place to carry a tomato, onion or mango when they appeared for sale on a street corner or one of the wheelbarrow-toting travelling sales people who went up and down every street, singing their offerings. "Freeesh bread, two pesos; carboooon!" Every person who sold the home-made cooking charcoal hollered the same way as they clopped up and down every street with their carretons. As a kid, Fidel would run behind them, mocking them with his own version of their advertising. He later realized he was just helping them to save their own vocal chords, and it wasn't as much fun anymore.

Realizing only about fifteen minutes had passed since he'd arrived, Fidel decided one prawn probably wouldn't fetch him two dollars. Probably more like fifty cents, and the television and washing machine were still about eight years away at this rate. This grown-up responsibility thing was not all that much fun, he decided, but he didn't care for the idea of spending his days in the hot sun chopping sugar cane with a machete, so he dried his eyes, pulled his goggles on, and waded back into the cold water. He thought about the scar he'd have on his finger to remind him of today, and decided to see if prawn one had any relatives in his cave.

As it turned out, there was something of a family reunion going on, and Fidel had crashed the party. He swiped his bandaged hand in and came out with a slightly smaller version of the alien, this time with its claw clamped over the finger completely, and not perforating his skin. There was some pain, but nothing like the first time, and now he took the time to twist the kitchen knife into the claw and pry it open. He remembered the way his cousin told him to make a quick cut behind the tentacles and it would die instantly. He opened the bag and stuffed in the second prawn, and went back down for its relatives from out of town.

His mother would know immediately he was lying. She could always tell, because he couldn't look her in the eyes and lie. Every time he came up with another sore finger and another alien creature for the bag, though, made him feel like he could tell her the truth and still come out ahead.

There was only a tiny piece of bread and half a tomato left, but they tasted like a feast of arroz congris, the famous black beans and rice, also referred to as moros and cristianos; and yucca and roasted pork they always had for the new year's/revolution party. Fidel would take his shift turning the pig on the spit over the charcoal fire, refusing the glass of rum his uncles always offered him in jest. Fidel smiled to himself as he recalled last year's party, when he was the only male still standing by three in the afternoon. The first bottle of rum was opened at five in the morning when the sound of pigs squealing the way they only did for one reason, filled the air around Trinidad. Fidel, the other Fidel, had allowed every family to raise a pig to help the food situation, and anyone who could hold off until December thirty-first without butchering it or selling it, stuck their sharpest knife into their pig to celebrate a new year and another year of survival in the stifling world of socialism.

The backpack was beginning to bulge by the time Fidel had cleaned out the last of the relatives from the reunion. He'd spotted a couple of other likely venues and decided he still had half an hour to hunt before he needed to head for the cobblestone streets to beat his mother home. The first rock had nothing under it. He decided some of the relatives from the reunion had lived there. The second, though, reminded him of the pain of the first victim, as a giant claw reached clear over the first finger and clamped into the second one. This time, though, he wasn't going to make it worse. He slipped out of the water, hobbling on his rear end, using his left hand as a crutch to get within reach of the knife, and stuck the sharp blade into its neck and felt the relief of the claw releasing its vice grip. This time, the blood didn't gush from the wound. It just turned the white plastic around his other finger a nice shade of pink. Fidel took a minute to enjoy this one – as prawns went, this one was a giant. He decided this one was going to be dinner on his own plate, and not the Aguila's.

A fast car roared across the bridge over his head. Must be a Yuma, he decided. Cubans didn't normally drive that fast so they would use less fuel. That brought on another one of his imaginings of a handsome foreigner falling madly in love with his beautiful mother and taking them away to live in a big house with carpet on the floor and roasted pork every day for breakfast and balls with air in them to play soccer… and the blond, blue-eyed girls who would fall in love with him.

Fidel glanced over at a cow that had wandered near the bridge; it stared back as it chewed the grass sticking out of both sides of its mouth. It seemed to be telling him to stop being so foolish – the tourists didn't go for the single mothers. There were plenty of young single girls to take care of the Yumas. The big, sad brown eyes looked so bored as the cow swished a swarm of insects from its exposed ribs. For some reason, Fidel recalled the clothes his mother had been wearing when she left for the Candonga – the name given to the handcraft market, after the local markets in Angola the soldiers frequented during the war Cuba joined there to defend Communism. No cleavage, he remembered. He was always worried someone would get the wrong idea when his mother showed her ample boobs. She liked to wear tight clothes, and wasn't shy about how great a body she had. He'd heard her laughing about the offers she'd received from men who wanted to buy more than a crocheted sweater. He wished he'd been there when they made their little comments to his mother. The David and Goliath rock in his pocket would have found its mark. The Cuban men made comments like that all the time, but they were different. Cuban men were naturally pigs, but the tourists were supposed to be different.

One more trip down to the giant's cave to see if he lived alone, and Fidel decided his day at the mines was over. There was just a sliver of ice left in his bottle, and he decided the river water was just as clean as what came out of their taps at home, and he dipped the bottle in to get enough for a long swallow. He wiped as much water off of himself as he could, and had a staring contest with the bored cow while he let the afternoon sun finish drying him.

When he'd finished pulling on his pants and shirt, and tied the broken laces of his mismatched tennis shoes, he reached for the backpack. He nearly lost his balance and had to do a two-step on the sharp rocks when he realized the weight of the nearly two dozen prawns he'd captured. At school, when they needed to raise funds for a project, like fixing the flag pole, the director always made a big deal out of painting a big arrow and pasting it on the door to her office, filling in the advancements at the end of every week. It made it more fun to bring the few pesos he could scrounge from his mother and grandparents. It felt like a personal victory when the arrow was completely painted. He wondered why the director sometimes had new shoes or cans of real pop for lunch, but she was the director – she must have been rich.

In his mind, Fidel painted in the bottom section of an arrow that pointed to a washing machine and television. The painted part was just a fine line, still, but Fidel decided he could do this every weekend and his mother would be able to stop washing his uniform on the washboard by the end of the summer.

He was climbing the bank up to the bridge when a flock of emerald-green parrots flew over his head; their distinct sound always grabbed his attention. He always thought they were talking about crackers in their own language. His grandfather had a parrot on his veranda that swore at every person who passed by on the street. Granddad laughed every single time. The people it swore at always shook their heads and laughed, too. He'd learned quickly that swearing like the parrot got him a sharp cuff behind the ears from the old coot, and if his mother heard him it was much worse – she would look at him as though she was disappointed, and that would bring on a flood from his tear ducts that he had to hide from anyone around.

His grandfather – well, technically it was his half-sister Sandra's grandfather, but she let Fidel call him grandpa, too, sold flowers and medicinal plants and avocados and mangos from his gigantic garden. Fidel sometimes helped serve the customers since his granddad limped from a sore knee he'd had since Fidel could remember. The flowers always drew hummingbirds, and Fidel knew from school lessons that the Cuban hummingbird was the smallest in the world. It was hardly bigger than a large bee, and the color was brilliant. He'd seen baby hummingbirds once, in a nest in the shed, and remembered how the babies' tongues seemed to be longer than their bodies as they reached for whatever their parents had brought them to eat.

He gauged the hour from the position of the sun as he crossed the bridge. He looked back down the highway towards Cienfuegos, the next city. He could see the mountains off to his right from Topes de Collante, the beautiful community where his father's family lived in the military apartments. Topes was like another world from Trinidad. High up in the mountains, it was so cold at night people had actual heaters in their homes. There were pine trees and squirrels and so many different birds that there were entire tours for the rich foreigners who paid money just to check off new species in their little bird books. His tenth birthday had been spent hiking one of the trails there that ended at a waterfall and swimming hole like they show in the movies. Maybe he'd use some of his money to take his mother there for her birthday, but it was coming up fast, so he'd need to hurry.

He nodded to the cow, and turned his attention to the long uphill walk ahead of him. It had been easy coming down, and his backpack had only carried a liter of water and half a sandwich and an avocado. Now it was at least two kilometers of hard walking, and his pack already pulled his shoulders back like his mother did when she wanted to improve his posture. He decided he'd have perfect posture by the time he got home, so his mother would be happy about that.

A big old Chevrolet chugged past him, going the opposite way. The diesel engine it sported now must have come from a smoke machine the way it filled the air with fumes and black fog. Miguel Enrique loved cars, and could spout off the make and model and year of everything on four wheels. At least Fidel assumed his cousin knew the make and model. He had no way of confirming or denying. He knew a car from a truck, and a truck from a tractor, but that was the extent of his car sense.

From somewhere behind him, Fidel heard the sound of a squeaking bicycle chain and a steady grunting. He turned in time to see what appeared to be a skeleton with clothes riding a bike that looked like it had been made from parts of a dozen different things, only a few of which had been bicycles. How this skinny old man could be actually riding it and pedaling, Fidel could not fathom. It must have weighed more than the Chevrolet that just passed him. He imagined the old fossil winning the Tour de France on a road bike. This would be the perfect training machine for Lance Armstrong, the American guy who had won the race seven times. He doubted that the relic who had just overtaken him had any hormones injected into him, either. Fidel laughed at the image of the needle going in one side of this guy's rear end and coming right out the front. Cubans weren't on the list of the countries with the most obesity. That was one thing to be proud of.

One of the things that made Cubans as great as they were was the way they could always find something to laugh at, always a positive spin, even in the most negative situation. Fidel Castro was the king of spinning. When Russia's economy hit a dead end, and they turned off the tap of funds to Cuba all at once, Fidel called the ensuing decade of austerity "The Special Period". Not, "We're REALLY up the creek," or "Assume crash positions"; he knew how to work it to the max. New programs came on the television showing people how to soak their rice for an extra day to make it twice as big, and how to add a little spice and color to grapefruit rinds so they'd look a little like a slice of pork. New weed soups were suddenly gobbled down by smiling children on the news, and Fidel could remember seeing the exact same footage of deliriously happy farm workers who proudly announced new records of production, month after month. The age-old question of which came first, the chicken or the egg, had a new twist – which got eaten first, the chicken or the egg. Chicken in the market for sale started to resemble pigeons for more than one reason. Mostly because they were actually pigeons being sold as chicken, but also because there was such a demand for food that no one waited for a chicken, or an onion, or a bean, to reach maturity. People who lived in the country were suddenly walking zombies – they couldn't sleep without waking up to an empty garden. Horses disappeared from their harnesses and became extra-red meat. The penalty for killing a cow for meat was suddenly much stiffer than killing a person. People with large cats had to keep them indoors, and people with large bellies suddenly became strangely attractive.

Fidel shook himself back to the present, realizing he'd made a serious calculation error, thinking the trip home would be roughly the same duration as the one to the river. He was only a third of the way up the hill, just about to the monument, and he knew he'd been walking for half an hour already. The prawns felt heavier than ever, now, and the thought of carrying food made him feel even hungrier than he already was. His mother told him he was like a steam engine, she had to constantly shovel more coal into him or he'd just stop moving. Stopping moving sounded beautiful at this moment. Unfortunately that wasn't an option. He had to speed up, and not just a little, or he wouldn't be home before dinner, and his finger wouldn't be the only part of him throbbing when his mother got a hold of him.

He felt like he was speeding up, but the distance to the top of the hill didn't look like it was diminishing very much at all. Maybe if he stopped to rest for a few minutes he could run the rest of the way up. He decided to try that method out and dropped his backpack on the shady side of the monument where he'd eaten half his sandwich only a few hours earlier. When he opened his eyes he could immediately identify two problems: the first was that the sun was about to drop into the ocean, meaning he'd fallen asleep for at least a couple of hours; and there were two very large and very ugly vultures sitting on the nearest fence posts. Thinking about what state his mother must be in by now, he decided he'd far prefer to tangle with the vultures. These hideously ugly birds had wing spans of over six feet, and had been known to cause serious damage to cars that couldn't get out of their way in time on the highways. There was a definite shortage of metal and glass between Fidel and the vultures, and they looked very hungry for the banquet he had in the pack he rested his head on.

From down the hill toward the curve that led to the river, he saw the shape of a horse and carreton heading his way. He wasn't supposed to take rides from strangers, but considering he was about to be dead from one of two fronts, torn to shreds on one side, and, well -- on both sides; he figured asking for a lift from a stranger wouldn't get him killed a second time. As it turned out, and usually did in a community that had been around for just shy of 500 years, there was a second degree connection between him and the carreton driver. When Fidel mentioned his father, the lobster diver, Carlos, his new friend, explained that he had been married to his father's Aunt Isabel many years earlier. He agreed to take him as far as the cemetery at the entrance to Trinidad, because he had to go the opposite way once he got there. That would take him to the top of the hill, and from there it would only be a fifteen minute walk home.

He spotted them as they rounded the curve that led into town, where the house with the flowers was. Two guys in their early twenties, riding those old road racing bikes with the curved handlebars. The cool guys stripped the bikes down to the bare necessities, and one of the things they didn't feel were necessary were brakes. He'd seen them before; they were modern day sharks on two wheels. They circled the entrance to Trinidad, watching for tourists in rental cars. They were easy to spot, since nobody else would be driving a car newer than 1959. They would stop the cars by whatever means necessary – usually by just blocking them and waving their arms in a friendly manner. They were the local welcome wagon, and spoke enough English or German or French to tell the driver there was some construction on the main street, and they could guide them to wherever they needed to get for a small fee. Their true motive, though, was to lure them down the specific streets where the lower classed bed and breakfasts (casa particular was the local name for them) would pay them a five dollar commission for every night these tourists stayed in their casas, and more for every meal they ate at inflated prices. Fidel knew all of this because his father sold lobster to these unregistered casas, and he heard them laughing about the prices they charged the unsuspecting Yumas. This was something Fidel hated to hear. He knew from his mother that their future depended on tourism, and if tourists felt cheated they wouldn't come back, and would tell more and more people in their countries.

He knew them, but they obviously didn't make the connection as to whose son he was. It wasn't thirty seconds from the time Carlos waved good-bye to him that the two of them circled around him like a pair of great whites, sizing up the potential.

Fidel tried to ignore them and walk faster, looking at the ground in front of him. He knew one of them was called Chichi. He was the one with the scar on his neck from a fight with a construction worker over a bottle of rum. Apparently the bottle won.

"Got something heavy in your pack for such a young guy," the other one said to him.

"I can handle it okay, thanks."

Chichi pulled his bike in close beside him and bumped the pack with his right knee. Fidel hiked it over to his other shoulder, out of reach. It was feeling extremely heavy, all of a sudden, probably from power of suggestion. He wished he could just drop it and run, but he hadn't spent the day tearing his hands into ribbons only to leave his treasure for someone else. He wished he'd taken after his father more, physically. Fidel was shorter than most of his friends at school, and too thin, he knew. Two injections a week at the policlinic for asthma kept him breathing normally, but he had no stamina for running or any kind of physical sports. His cousin Miguel Enrique looked like Superman compared to him. He and his buddies spent all of their free time lifting weights and doing every kind of exercise they could think of. Fidel swept the house from front to back every afternoon after school. That was his exercise program.

"Where you coming from, anyway?" the first guy asked. The two of them were forming a wheeled gate for him, now, one on each side of him.

Fidel figured he needed to use his trump card right away. "I'm taking this pack of prawns to a restaurant for my dad, Ergeny, the lobster diver." He felt the change in the air immediately. There was a look exchanged between them. He was pretty sure there weren't two Ergeny's who dove for lobster. Well, actually there were – his father and his brother -- but he knew that nobody messed with his father. He'd been a wrestler in school, and had a reputation as a tough guy. It was probably more economics than fear that changed their plans for Fidel. They enjoyed the commissions from the lobster dinners the tourists paid dearly for, and Ergeny brought most of the lobster. Instead of being an easy mark, they dropped back from beside him to confer out of earshot, and just when Fidel thought they were going to turn back to their regularly scheduled programming, Chichi pulled up beside him and stopped. His voice and demeanor were completely different now that he was talking to the son of a business partner.

"It's kind of dangerous for you to be carrying that stuff after dark. There are some bad guys around here."

Fidel just stared back into his eyes, letting him know his statement was the very definition of irony.

"If you tell me which restaurant, I could take the stuff there for you, and my friend could give you a ride home, since he's got the rack on his bike."

"Hey, Chichi," Fidel responded, letting him know he knew exactly who he was talking to. "I'll let my dad know you offered to help when I see him later. And tell your friend thanks, anyway, but I'm enjoying the walk."

They finally decided there was no win for them in this game, so with a nod from Chichi, the two of them turned back to the tourist trap business.

In the house on the corner he knew there was a phone. It was his sister's grandfather, the one who sold flowers. The problem was the only phone on his own street was at the Aguila's, and they didn't call anyone to the phone after six o'clock, and he knew it was well after six by now. It was only fifteen or so blocks home, anyway, so he didn't really see the advantage of letting the entire neighborhood know what he'd been up to. In Cuba there were more prying eyes than anything else. There wasn't much else to do but gossip and watch to see what everyone else was doing. It was the real national sport, not baseball, as some thought.

He didn't make it to his block before one of the neighbor kids spotted him from a few blocks away, and Fidel watched him run toward his house. He wasn't sure whether he preferred to speed up or slow down. Hell was waiting to break loose, and he had no good excuse for where he'd been or what he'd been doing. He was twelve years old, but his mother still wanted to hold his hand to cross the street, and wouldn't let him ride the neighbors' bicycles because he was surely going to ride them straight under a bus. His school, Jose Mendoza, was two blocks away, and she still walked him to the entrance and more often than not was waiting when he was ready to come home. Fidel thought about how he'd never had to suffer as his friends did with the free lunch at school. His mother had pulled strings and used her wide connections to justify that Fidel's asthma and sensitive stomach made it necessary for him to bring his own lunch to school every day. He almost wished he knew what the watery rice and stale beans tasted like. That was part of the experience of school life in Cuba, and it had passed him by.

Before he could see her face, he could distinguish his mother by her stance: she stood halfway down the block from their house, one hand on her hip and the other on her forehead, just over her left eye. That was how she stood when

72

she was nursing a particularly painful headache. More often than not her headaches had a first name and a last name: Fidel Rodriguez. She used to tell him when he was younger that all of her problems were because of somebody named Fidel. People always laughed quietly. Everyone knew it was dangerous to even speak a negative word about their revered commandant. She had an excuse, and used it to her advantage when she could. "Oh, Fidel, Fidel, Fidel... what have you done now?"

When he got close enough, she grabbed him and pulled him to her chest, where he felt his tears spreading in the cloth on her worn blue t-shirt she'd worn around the house for as long as he could remember. It had the letters and heart that said "I love New York." A Yuma had given it to her in the market when she first started there. Over the years, it had been her best shirt to go out for dinner or to the annual carnival, but as it faded and the letters wrinkled and began to disappear, it went from her going out shirt to her hanging out shirt to her cleaning the house shirt, which it was now.

She knew more about avoiding the eyes of the "chismosos" than most, and marched her son past the small group that had gathered, waiting for the fireworks. She deliberately closed the door to the street, and snapped shut the wooden slat shutters that were always left open for the breeze they allowed into the tiny house.

She showed him to one of the wicker rockers that faced the wall where a television might be, and went to the kitchen where she chipped ice into two glasses of boiled and filtered water. She found her stash of medicine and popped a Duralgina pain pill out of the bubble wrap package. She looked at it for a few seconds, and decided to add a second. She tipped her head back and swallowed the tablets and drained the glass. Fidel watched her methodically wash and dry the glass and set it back on the glass shelf above the chipped sink. Then she seemed to turn into soft modelling clay, and had to hold herself from crumbling to the floor with both hands on the cement block counter. She lowered her head and looked away from him, and started to cry. He saw her shoulders wiggle up and down as they did when she cried silently in her bed and didn't want him to know.

Now the backpack on the floor beside the door looked smaller than it felt on his shoulders just a few minutes before. The weight in his chest was heavier now, seeing how he'd made his mother cry once again. He glanced at the bare wall where the television he'd wanted to buy would have been. The back wheel of her Russian bike protruded from the doorway of the space they used as a bedroom. He could see the outline of the textile of the tires where the treads were worn so smooth that they spun if she tried to pedal too hard on the loose gravel. The pile of dirty clothes that would be washed by hand again sat on the edge of the bed they both used.

Fidel felt his eyes fill with tears for the third or fourth time that day, and was glad his cousin Miguel Enrique wasn't there to see it. It wasn't for pain, though, so his cousin wouldn't say he was a baby. It was because he knew he'd disappointed his mother, and she didn't deserve to be disappointed. He just wished she'd yell at him and punish him and get it over with. He didn't want a television anymore, or anything else for that matter. He wanted his mother to be happy and smiling and laughing and dancing again like she used to.

Finally, he saw her draw a deep breath and wipe her eyes. She glanced over at him, and he saw her eyes fall onto his hands, still covered with little home-made plastic bandages. He tried to cover his right hand with his left, but it was too late.

She didn't yell at him, though. Instead, she looked at him with such adoration and concern that it made his tears flow even more.

"I wanted to help you buy a washing machine," he managed, as she took his damaged hand in hers. "And a color television."

She didn't respond, just held his hand up to her lips and kissed each and every wound, tears coming from her beautiful eyes like the river he'd been diving in a few hours earlier.

"I have something that'll make these feel better," she said, referring to his wounded fingers. "Your father came home almost every night the same way."

"Aren't you gonna punish me, or yell at me?"

"From the smell coming from that bag, I'm guessing you've decided to follow in his footsteps, and there was no amount of yelling that could change who he was."

"Is that why you and my father got divorced?"

"No, honey… your father and I didn't get divorced because of who he was. He was a diver long before I met him, and he'll be diving for many more years to come."

Fidel waited for further explanation. It didn't come for a few minutes, as his mother seemed to look at something far away before she spoke again.

"I loved your father very much, no matter what he did for a living. The problem was he never really knew what he wanted, but whatever it was it included taking advantage of the young women who were charmed by his good looks and the way he made everything into a party. I wanted more of what we have here, you and me. A happy home, enough to eat every day, and maybe a picnic at the beach on Sunday mornings. Boring."

Already his fingers felt better as his mother worked the salve into the cracks and cuts. Fidel glanced over at the pack, and the little wet puddle that had formed where the seam touched the floor.

"Did you catch a lot of prawns?"

He allowed himself to flash a smile, finally.

"Did I ever! There're twenty-five in there. Twenty-four to sell and one for us for dinner."

"Let's sell twenty-three this time," she smiled, shoving his shoulder playfully. "I want a big one all to myself."

Fidel jumped to his feet and raced over to show her his haul.

He carried the pack to the rough counter in the kitchen and dumped them into a big plastic pan to wash them and get them ready.

"Do you think you could show me how to clean them?"

"Obviously! You don't think I'm gonna do all this work myself!" She flashed him another long look when she saw he'd taken her best knife with him. His smile faded as he waited for another lashing of her sharp tongue. "Well, you weren't gonna cut these monsters open with a butter knife, now were you?"

Maria grabbed the biggest one, and he grabbed a smaller one, expecting the lesson in cleaning to begin. Instead, she propped the claw open with her forefinger and shoved it into his face, roaring at him as if it was the alien from the movie on Saturday night. Fidel jumped back from the surprise, but was quick to find his own monster voice and battled the big one with his smaller, faster, smarter version.

The meal of the two prawns was the best Fidel could ever remember. He ate every morsel of his, and the part of his mother's she said she couldn't finish because it was so big.

His mother helped him clean and prepare the rest of them and sent him with the bag to the Aguila's, three doors down. She had weighed them already, so he knew the price. There would be nearly 800 Cuban pesos added to the jar for a day's work. Not bad at all.

When he returned he found his mother scrounging in the storage space above the washing rack in the back yard. She pulled out an old box Fidel didn't remember ever having seen before. In it there was an ancient snorkel and set of fins.

"Are these my father's?" he asked, as she wiped the dust from them.

"They're mine," Maria responded. "Where did you think I met your father, anyway?"

Fidel looked at his mother in a completely different manner. He had no idea she even knew how to dive.

From the bottom of the box, she fished out a small medallion tied with a ribbon. Fidel grabbed it from her hands.

"First place, lobster fest, 2002," he read the medallion out loud.

"Your father came in third," she winked at him. "Didn't I tell you there was salt water in your veins?"

ERGENY
SR

Father of the Year

Ergeny felt the pain of every cobblestone. This time the gout was worse than he'd ever recalled. The ball of his left foot felt like the nerves had been exposed and every step was excruciating. This was supposed to be the rich man's illness – from too much red wine and red meat. The last time he'd been in crisis, the international pharmacy had traded him the injection of Diclofenaco for two medium-sized lobsters, but when he'd stopped by there earlier in the week, when he first felt the pain, there hadn't been any in Trinidad in more than two months, the guy had told him.

He lifted his left foot up and leaned against one of the upside-down cannons that decorated many of the street corners of the "Historic Center" of Trinidad. Most of the locals called it the "Hysteric Center", with all of the vendors trying to grab every peso they could from the Yumas. Between the bed and breakfasts and the private restaurants, the tourists couldn't walk three steps without having someone pounce on them. These were Ergeny's bread and butter, though – they bought more lobster in a day than he provided to the government in a month. He'd just come from one, now – Yamile and Pedro Arturo's place. They'd taken ten kilos of tails and a dozen of the river prawns, and wanted more for the group coming the following week.

He'd winced when Yamile had grabbed him around the neck to reach up to hug him. He'd half-lost his balance and placed all of his weight on his left foot, and BOOM... almost lights out! This was supposed to happen to old guys, not young men in the prime of their lives. Well, maybe his prime was a few years behind him, but not that far back.

A couple of bici-taxis bounced past him, and he considered hiring one to take him home, but he didn't like to spend money if he had the time to spare. He was done for the night – well, done work, anyway. He'd promised Claudia he'd meet her before he went home. She had something she needed to talk to him about. When she needed to talk to him, that meant she needed money for something. It was always money. She needed shoes, or her mother had no medicine, or her brother needed some book or other for university in Santa Clara. The problem was she wasn't anything to him but a little fun at the end of the day, before he got home to the crying baby and complaining wife number four.

It made him wish he could curb his habit of flashing his perfect white teeth and perfect green dollars at every young thing that passed in front of him. He heard once sex could be an addition, just like drugs or alcohol, so that had cemented it for him – it wasn't his fault – he was addicted to sex. Of course it was only sex with women who weren't married to him. That had to have been a special mutation of the addiction. Looking back over twenty years and four marriages, he'd definitely slept with more women outside of the vows than inside.

Ergeny tried to plant his foot, testing it after the rest. Like always, it was worse. The first time he put his weight on it was always the hardest. It was like offering the cheek for the nurse to stab the needle into, knowing the pain came after she'd removed it, when the antibiotics were pulsing into the muscle. He was a man, though, and with his barrel chest and muscular arms and legs from a lifetime of diving and fighting for respect in the Barranca, he couldn't very well avoid walking the five blocks to the house Claudia always borrowed from her wealthy aunt who was visiting Miami.

When he saw the familiar silhouettes of Chichi and Joseito approaching on their old bikes with the bald tires, he knew they were looking for their commissions for the order from Yamile. They had a sixth sense about their commissions. They could smell them from five miles away. He'd already separated their two dollars and forty cents. Yamile always had plenty of change on hand from selling single cigarettes on the side. That gave him an idea.

"Chichi, I was just looking for you," Ergeny lied.

"Funny, I thought maybe you were about to run the other way."

Ergeny chuckled to himself. If he could have even walked, he might have avoided these creeps, at least for a day or two. It was debatable, though, who made more money for whom. Sort of the chicken and egg question. They were in touch with all of the b&b's and private restaurants, and got him lots of business he'd never have had for his lobster and other fish, but these guys probably had the best business in Trinidad. Pure profit, with no work and no risk. They never got caught carrying bags of iced lobster tails or stinking prawns and shrimp in the street. They didn't have to borrow hundreds of dollars from relatives in Miami to renovate their houses into b&b's, and then pay horrendous taxes to the government and more to the cabrones inspectors who could always find a reason to fine them at least half of what they took in. They didn't have to steal bottles of rum and cigars from the factories and all-inclusive hotels to resell on the street. They were just the middle men – pointing the customers at the suppliers who paid them the most commissions. Their old bikes with the bald tires and no brakes were just their work clothes. Chichi had a great house in La Boca, looking out at the ocean, and had an old Chevy that was being fitted with a new diesel engine he'd paid close to five thousand dollars for. Joseito, on the other hand, was far too fond of good rum and bad women – he rode the old bike because he had no choice. It didn't matter much, though. He was bald because of the chemo treatments, and Ergeny had heard they weren't doing much good.

Ergeny counted off the dollar twenty to each of them, and convinced Chichi to take Joseito home on his back rack, so he could use the bike, just for tonight. He'd drop it off before noon the next day, or Joseito could pick it up in the Barranca if he needed it any sooner. Chances are he'd still be drunk by noon, anyway. Terminal cancer had been Joseito's reason to curl up with his favorite Havana Club Siete Años every night. He figured liver failure might be less painful than rotting from the inside out.

Even peddling the piece of crap bike was more than Ergeny had bargained for. Murphy's Law had conspired to make the left pedal the one that didn't swivel right, and every bounce on the cobble-stone streets reminded him of how much he appreciated asphalt. He'd left his own bike at home to save it and the tires for his next trip to the beach the following day. New tires for his mountain bike were going for nearly twenty-five dollars each, and he needed two of them. The next turtle he bagged was pegged for two new tires. Theresa, his latest wife, had some other things in mind the next time any money came home – they were all things that she was sure Edith needed – clothes, creams, a bigger crib, a stroller – the list went on forever. That was the problem now with all of the tourists coming around with their new toys. Now everybody wanted the same things. Needed them, they said. Sandra, his first daughter had never had a stroller or a crib, and she'd turned out just fine. He considered what Theresa would think if she knew about the bank accounts he deposited money into every month.

He saw Claudia's knees before he saw the rest of her. She was sitting on the steps of her aunt's big old colonial house, visiting with another girl about her age who he'd seen before. He contemplated the events that were about to transpire, remembering how great those legs, and everything else about her, were. Claudia had actually been two years behind Theresa in the same high school, and they had been friends, though not close. She didn't seem to mind at all that he was married, or that she knew his wife. She told him once, in the heat of the moment, that it made it all the more exciting for her. A month earlier, Ergeny had stepped into the TRD shop to pick up batteries and had bumped right into Claudia and Theresa, and the two of them were goofing around with little Edith. Claudia had actually winked at him. That was just not right.

When she leaned forward and confirmed the approaching cyclist was Ergeny, the friend said her good-byes and turned toward him to walk home. She locked her eyes onto his and smiled a little more than was appropriate, and continued on. He couldn't help himself, and looked back to take a mental picture of the Spandex shorts that left nothing at all to the imagination. He knew she had kicked her hips into high gear, on the chance he'd be looking. "What was in the water?" Ergeny mused to himself. "They just keep getting better and better."

Claudia rose to meet him as he jabbed his right toe in between the front fork and the tire, making his own brake pad from his worn Adidas. She had the doors open, letting in some fresh air. Her aunt left her the key when she went to Miami every couple of years, and Claudia made sure to clean it before she returned. In the meantime, she had her own private five star suite. Her aunt had most of her family in Miami since the time of the revolution, and she had never had to worry about money. Her brother had been a lawyer for more than thirty years in the States, and helped her to amass an impressive collection of antiques and valuable art. They planned to hold onto it until things opened up and they could make a fortune. They were both in their seventies, now, and the opening up wasn't anywhere on the horizon, yet. Claudia made it her life's work to fall all over her aunt so that she would be the chosen heir. For now, though, she was happy to have a great bed to have sex in whenever she got the urge, and hot and cold water in the shower.

Ergeny didn't like to waste any time in the street, so he hobbled the bike through the double doors and propped it against a four-hundred-year-old wash stand with the matching porcelain basin and wash jug. Claudia's aunt would not have approved, but then again, she was an old spinster who had never had even a boyfriend, so there were a lot of things going on in her house that she wouldn't have approved of, he was sure.

Claudia had made coffee while she'd waited for him. Her aunt had a fancy automatic coffee maker, and she loved to use it. All they had at home was a manual aluminum pot that unscrewed in the middle and the coffee percolated as the water boiled. Theirs was older than she was, though, and there was more steam coming through the threads than the top. She served Ergeny in a tiny cup that still had the finger holder on it, which was a rarity in Cuba, and a matching little plate. Anyone who had such a thing in Trinidad reserved it as a decoration for their kitchen and only used them when a special visitor arrived. Once, when they had entertained a couple of Canadian tourists, they had borrowed plates, cutlery, glasses, cups, even four chairs that matched. One of the tourists bumped over his glass, and she told him how she and her parents had held their breath, wondering how they could replace it had it broken, which thankfully, it hadn't.

When he'd finished the two-step process of drinking coffee (one sip to test the flavor and temperature, and a second gulp to finish it off), she carefully washed the tiny dishes and returned them to their exact location on the glass shelf above the coffee maker. Ergeny watched her movements – something was just a little off from her normal jovial self. She usually had her arms around him by this time, doing her best to rev up his engine. Tonight, though, she was being extra domestic.

"Something up?" Ergeny finally asked her, pulling her attention from the shelf she was wiping with her cloth.

"What do you mean?" Claudia responded, maybe just a little too fast.

"That's what I mean," he said, referring to the cloth in her hand. "You know I don't have time to play house. I have to get home before the baby is asleep."

Claudia's shoulders dropped, and she slumped back against the sink.

"No sense dragging this out," she started, but her lip began to tremble before she could continue.

"What is it? Is it your mother? Is she sick, again?"

"I'm pregnant." She figured if she didn't spit it out all at once, she wouldn't be able to. "Nearly six weeks."

Ergeny's gout just became the best part of his day. Not this, again. He couldn't deal with this tonight. Maybe if he went home and got a good night's sleep, when he woke up this would have been another bad dream.

"So, I guess you want me to help you to take care of this, you know…"

Claudia looked up at him as she assimilated what he was saying. Her eyes narrowed.

"No, Ergeny… I'm not 'taking care of it'. It's my baby and I'm going to have it. I love you, and I would never do anything to harm our child."

Ergeny held up his hand to signal Claudia to stop her speech. "First of all, you don't love me – you have no idea what love is, yet, but I can tell you for sure it isn't what you feel for me. And second, I have a vote in this, too. I've got a hell of a lot more at stake here than you do."

Claudia looked angry now, offended by Ergeny's assumption she wasn't old enough to know if she loved him or didn't. She had thought of nothing else since she'd come back from the visit to the clinic a few days earlier with the confirmation of her suspicions in hand. Her friend Yudelsy – Pollo to her friends – had told her point blank she needed to get rid of the baby and find a boyfriend who wasn't married. Based on the way she had smiled at him on her way past earlier, Ergeny considered the possibility she just wanted him for herself. Young girls were funny that way.

How many times did this scenario need to play itself out? He was running out of women who weren't related to each other. This city was getting far too small for him, and it just shrunk a whole lot more with this news.

Ergeny knew that his reputation as a love-em and leave-em jerk was growing by the day. He could understand it, naturally, since he'd had one child with each of his wives, and then moved on to the next younger model. They'd never understand, and he couldn't tell them anyway, so he just had to take their commentaries and the hatred of all of his fathers-in-law in stride. It was far better than the alternative.

"If you have this baby, I won't help you with it. I've got four children of my own that I don't do nearly enough for."

Claudia had obviously prepared her speech, "I'm not keeping this baby for you. I'm keeping it for me. This is MY baby, MY body, and MY decision." She couldn't hold back the flood of tears, now.

Ergeny moved to take a step toward her to calm her, and was stopped less by the pain in his foot than by the look of indifference Claudia gave him. He had just died to her. Instead of trying to console her, he knew the best thing he could do was to turn the bicycle around and go home.

He almost welcomed the excruciating pain in his foot as he wrestled the bike down the steps. The right pedal caught the ancient door as he passed, and he saw a piece of four-hundred-year-old wood splinter onto the green tile step. Perfect way to end the night, he thought to himself.

He thought about riding the bike against the one-way traffic, but he'd been caught more times than he'd care to remember, and chose to walk it the block-and-a-half to the main street that led to the Barranca. It wasn't the fine that scared him. That he made back with every lobster he caught, three times over. It was the points they accumulated – once he had twenty-four points on his record, they'd seize his mountain bike for two or three months, and without transportation, it was a long way to the ocean and back. Last time they'd taken it away, it came back with a different set of gears and the brake cable had vanished into thin air. Cuba, beautiful Cuba.

He finally slipped the bike into the space behind the door, next to his own. There was still a tiny chunk of the wood from the aunt's door lodged in the pedal.

Theresa was asleep in the rocking chair in the front entry, with little Edith beside her in the little make-shift bed with the fan blowing on her little perfect face. Something about the fan triggered a memory of the one he'd received as a gift from Dalila's parents on their wedding day, four lifetimes ago. There were still a few limp balloons hanging from the little crib from her first birthday party, a few months earlier. That had been when he'd met Claudia.

He found a comfortable position on the wicker couch – well, what wicker was left in it, anyway. He reminded himself to call his friend Rodolfo to come over and rethread it before somebody fell through and hurt themselves. He could see the look on Theresa's face – fatigue mixed with anger and frustration – he knew she knew about Claudia. This town was way too small for her not to know. Probably didn't know she was knocked up, yet, but that wouldn't take long to come to the surface, literally. He reached over and pulled a cotton thread from Edith's cheek that was dancing to the breeze from the fan every time it passed in its trajectory. All of his children were beautiful – he couldn't deny that. But the mixture of her mother's dark black skin and his white skin, at least under the dark brown leather tan, made for a perfect little mulata. She'd be the prettiest of them all, he was sure.

He watched her breath, and saw how her little eyes moved under her eyelids, like she was watching a movie in her dreams. He wanted to pick her up and hold her to his chest and smell her baby smells. Innocent, pure, perfect. He was already contemplating how she'd fair in school – her mother was smart – she'd go to Jose Mendoza, where he'd gone, and two of his other kids went. He thought about the day in October when she would receive her first blue panuelo, handkerchief, around her neck. There'd be a speech from the director of the school, some kind of special treats brought by some of the mothers, and the picture for the wall. He'd seen the other pictures in his other children's houses – always with their proud mother beside them. In some of the other houses he'd visited, the pictures were taken with both parents. Ergeny had never been around long enough to take a child to school. Edith would one day have a picture like that one, probably on the wall next to where she was sleeping now, but he knew the only person in the picture with her would be Theresa.

He squeezed his eyes and wiped a tear with the back of his wrist. Better not to think about it. They're all better off without him than they would be with him. By the time this little angel was old enough to know who her father was, he'd be long gone. When she was twenty-one she'd learn about the money he'd start depositing soon. Sandra would be the first to find out she had enough money to pay for a better house; she'd just never know where it had come from. Then Ergeny, even though he probably needed it the least, but he could use it to help his mother more than he already did. Little Fidel was a good kid – not as big and strong as Ergeny – but just as determined. He smiled when he thought about how he'd gone down to the river not long before to dive for prawns. That took guts. His nephew Miguel Enrique had filled him in on the details, and told him about the scars Fidel still sported on his hand. Looking at his own hands, Ergeny could scarcely make out the scars under the scars under the scars. He remembered the first time, though. You don't forget the first time one of those buggers latches on and you yank it off without thinking.

He would not repeat the sins of his father. Period.

He finally touched Theresa on the shoulder, to tell her she should move to the bed, or she'd suffer the next day from the shoulder pain she dealt with ever since the accident with the carreton when she was a little girl. She blinked herself into the present, and gave Ergeny a quick look, admonishing him for being so late, and then it was gone.

"Help me carry Edith and the fan to the bedroom, while I warm your dinner." She always had food prepared for him, no matter what time of the day or night he came home. Ergeny never ate in the street; not because he didn't like to spend money, but he had a weak stomach, and not knowing where the food came from, or how it was prepared always made it impossible for him to swallow anything not prepared in his own kitchen.

Ergeny's stomach responded to the news, reminding him he hadn't touched any food since he'd left before four in the morning to catch the hotel workers' bus to the all-inclusive hotels on the Ancon Peninsula. Technically, non-hotel personnel weren't allowed on the buses, but since he knew almost everyone who worked at any of the three hotels, including the bus drivers, they made an exception for him. It wasn't out of their way, anyway. He just hopped off when they slowed to take the corner that led to the peninsula, and he walked the half mile to his favorite dive spot. It wasn't actually a beach, since this part of the coast had been pounded by the waves for so long that any sand had been washed away. All that was left was the porous volcanic rock that looked more like a big, black sponge than a beach. That was one of the reasons Ergeny liked it there –

because other people *didn't* like it there. He wasn't much interested in what the shoreline looked like, or how comfortable it was to lay out in the sun on a towel drinking fruity beverages. He liked what he saw when he was under the water, and that was plenty of coral and big rocks and other natural hiding places for lobster and other exotic fish. He usually carried three old plastic bottles of frozen water, his diving gear and a little bait to get started with. The rest he'd catch fresh.

Theresa brought him a plate of three chicken legs in the tomato, garlic, and onion sauce they called fricase. She'd even found some potatoes to add to it – a rarity in Trinidad. She served it over a bed of the special Cuban rice and bean combination that had half a dozen names, but it was good, whatever it was called. Cumen was the spice of choice in Cuba, and knowing how much to put in was the difference between success and failure in the kitchen. Theresa was the hands-down winner in that department. She'd grown up in a four-generation house-hold, and was cleaning rice before she was three years old, and could peel a string of garlic faster than he'd ever seen. She loved the kitchen, and he loved to eat, so they made a great combination. He also didn't see color like so many others he knew. He loved women, and black, white or brown – it didn't matter one bit to him. Theresa was from a very pure African heritage. Very little mixture in her family, so she had a dark chocolate complexion that he loved. She came from a family of Santeros – highly respected by some, deathly feared by others. She'd grown up around it, and knew her way around a cigar and bottle of rum. She'd seen her grandmother writhing on the floor in a hypnotic frenzy while dozens of others in white clothes and colored beads chanted in tongues. Ergeny met her during one of those religious "events". Theresa was in the street, swaying and moving to the music in a way that stopped him in his tracks and held him there until he could get her attention. She was only seventeen at the time, and he was still married to Fidel's mother, Maria. It may have been the emotion of the Santeria adrenaline, but that night with her had been the most exciting of his life. She seemed to know him – really, really know him. She saw through his smile and charisma and reached right into his chest and grabbed his heart. When he was getting up to leave after making love to her that night, she stopped him in his tracks.

"Your father forgives you," she had said, point blank. He'd never mentioned his father to her, or anyone else, for that matter. His father was dead. Had been since he was fourteen years old.

He hadn't imagined he wanted his father's forgiveness for anything, but he'd almost lost the use of his legs when she'd said it, like she had some control over him. She knew things. He hadn't waited to find out she was pregnant before leaving Maria. He didn't care. He couldn't be around her when Fidel was old enough to know him as a father, so he'd packed his few things and left the very next day, and Theresa's family welcomed the white stranger into their world. They had an old place in the Barranca that nobody lived in, so he and Theresa brought her few things and he fixed the plumbing and electrical, and it was home. He still needed to fix a lot of leaks in the roof, but first he needed to keep the deposits in the other three bank accounts current. He was thankful that Vilma, the bank manager, lived only a few houses away, and he could just give her cash and she knew to divide it between the three accounts. She never took a dime for herself, even though he always offered. She didn't protest, though, when a couple of nice fish showed up on her doorstep.

"The fricase was great. Thanks, Tere." Ergeny tried to make Theresa feel better, knowing she had more on her own plate than anyone her age needed. She could see the end of their marriage long before he could. She'd probably hit up her family to cast some terrible Santeria spell on him. He wasn't a big believer in that stuff, but he sure did respect it. He'd seen some pretty weird stuff go on and even found different kinds of powders and dead birds and animal blood around his diving stuff. Over the years, plenty of people had wanted bad things for him. Most of them had been justified. Probably three ex-wives had all called on their saints to do damage to his genitals. Thankfully that was one part of him that hadn't been affected, yet. Obviously, with the news from

Claudia, it was a shame the voodoo stuff hadn't worked.

She had a pot on the old hotplate, heating up water for his bath. He rubbed his sore foot while he watched her in the kitchen. She was very business-like in there, he noticed. No singing or dancing – she flipped open tins of spices and grabbed pinches of this and that. Nothing was labelled. He had no idea where to find anything in there, but she did. She had the little bowl out with the tiny baseball bat, crushing something into a paste while she tossed a palm-full of salt into his bath water. He could smell the paste from the living room, and recognized it as the balm she had massaged into his foot the previous time his gout was in crisis, before he got the shot of Diclofenaco. She took good care of him, this one. He was really going to miss her.

His exhaustion finally got the best of him, and he crumpled to the floor in the doorway between the bedroom and the kitchen. What did she really know about his father, he wondered as he lost consciousness?

It was still dark when Ergeny's eyes flung open, checking to see where he was. He'd taken enough whacks on the head for calling out the wrong wife's name, so he always made a note to figure out where he was before saying his first words. Theresa was already in the rocking chair bottle feeding little Edith, and there was a bag on the counter that looked familiar in size. She'd have filled and frozen his three green bottles with water she boiled and filtered for him. There'd be half a dozen boiled eggs that she got from the family hen-house, and half of the loaf of bread, left over from the morning before. She soaked it in the leftover sauce from the chicken she'd made him the previous night, and would leave the avocado whole, so it wouldn't turn black on the journey. Two tomatoes, and a little bag of salt to add once he'd made the sandwich – it wasn't so much that she was predictable as observant. She'd seen him prepare for his diving trips a couple of times, and when she saw that he packed the same thing each time, she just took over and did it. She was going to make some lucky guy a fantastic wife, he mused, noticing the sticky mess on his swollen foot. He tested his weight on it, and shook his head involuntarily at the realization that the severe pain had dissipated through the few hours he'd been asleep. He didn't have to ask how he'd gotten from the floor to the bed. He just had. He didn't want to know if she'd conjured up some spirit from the past that had picked him up and carried him to the bed and dressed his aching foot.

Theresa had even oiled the chain on his bicycle sometime before he'd woken. If he could just teach her to dive for lobster, he chuckled to himself. He was going to kiss her on his way out, but just as he approached, Theresa lifted Edith and changed from one shoulder to the other. He had received his response to whether she was angry with him or not. She showed so little emotion it was sometimes hard to tell. When she decided to raise a scandal, though, she knew how.

Ergeny accepted his penance, reached for the barracuda-tooth chain he'd received as a gift from Sandra. He only wore it when he dove, choosing to keep it safely-guarded the rest of the time. It was one of his most-treasured possessions in the world. Correction, it was his only treasured possession. Everything else belonged to the wives, past and present. And future? He thought about that, and decided there would definitely be no wife number five. Claudia could have the baby if she chose to, but he wouldn't share a roof with her – not even if the rich old aunt gave the place to her.

On his way out, he remembered to leave fifteen dollars on the little table by the door. He hadn't gotten a chance to pick up all of the things Theresa had asked for the day before, so he knew she'd get her nine-year-old brother Ricardito to pick them up. He loved feeling rich, going from store to store with a fist-full of Chavitos, the convertible currency they used in the shops. There was always some treat for himself, but nothing extravagant. He was a good kid. He studied hard. Shame about being half-blind. The glasses he wore only helped make him look more like a nerd than he was, but he couldn't see enough to even ride a bike on the street. He trotted everywhere he went, like he was riding his trusty steed. And how he loved his niece... he would come by after school every day just to play with her and help his sister take care of her.   He couldn't pronounce Edith, correctly, so he called her Deedee.

The trip to the beach was downhill from the Barranca, past the cemetery and Sandra's grand-father's flower market, so he could coast and save his energy for the long uphill climb towards La Boca, the little ocean-front community that tripled in population during the summer vacations, when everybody who could, which usually meant the families of military personnel, booked into the horrific rental rooms that surrounded the filthy pool. The beach wasn't much better, there, but the good beaches were all off limits, reserved for the Yumas who paid in Chavitos, not the tattered old Cuban pesos. Ergeny could have slept on the way to his diving spot, he'd been there so many times over the years. He knew every pot-hole and fence post on the way, and had often come home after dark without a problem.   He knew the places where the trouble-makers hid with their little ropes to catch cyclists off guard and rob their bicycles and whatever else they had with them. Somewhere one of those little buggers had a nasty scar on his arm and some missing teeth – Ergeny wasn't one to be messed with, especially sporting thirty or forty dollars' worth of lobster. He'd like to catch him one more time, in the act.

From La Boca to his dive spot was another long climb.   It wasn't steep, or anything, but steady, with no lulls. The Captain's house was always his milestone – once he passed the great place on his right – the place he always said he wanted to buy one day – he knew he was on the home stretch. He was always ready to tip up the shade he'd made months before and drain the melted water out of all three of the bottles. He had to be careful not to give himself a brain-freeze, drinking too much, too fast. That left them about three quarters full of pure ice, and it seemed to last longer that way. He'd peel one of the eggs and squash it onto the bread, and pull out his trusty diving knife (okay, two treasured possessions) and carve the avocado and tomatoes just the right thickness so they covered every bit of the surface of the bread. Then he'd poke a hole in the little plastic bag of salt and pour on twice the amount he should. He had salt in his blood from more than one source, he justified to himself.

He liked this ritual, doing the same thing each time, before going through the process of pulling on his dive suit, checking the elastic straps of the spear gun, and carrying the fins, mask and snorkel with him to his favorite natural step into the Batea, or washboard, as the spot had come to be known. On days when the ocean was rough, more than one person had been pounded onto the rocks, shredded into hamburger meat by the sharp, irregular edges of the volcanic surface. It earned its name on more than one occasion that Ergeny recalled. His nephew Miguel Enrique had almost perished there one afternoon when he got too confident and didn't get out of the water when he was told to. Had Ergeny not been there to scream instructions at him to grab the rocks no matter how much it hurt, he'd wouldn't have had the strength for one more attempt, and Ergeny would most likely have died trying to save him, because he wouldn't have let his nephew die alone. Miguel Enrique hadn't been back to the Batea since, and the scars on his chest and neck would remind him to listen to his old uncle the next time.

It wasn't yet six o'clock in the morning when Ergeny spit into his face mask and rubbed it into every crevice of the glass. He couldn't help but look to the south, toward the Costa Sur hotel with its natural swimming pool made from hauling giant rocks and depositing them in a semi-circle to break the waves from the open ocean. There, on the back side of the biggest rock formation, he'd had his final confrontation with his father. He'd been fourteen years old, nearly twenty years ago, when his old man laid his hands on Ergeny for the last time.

Drowned. Must've fallen and hit his head, the cops figured. No other reason they could think of. Luckily for Ergeny, one of the things they didn't think of was that he'd wrestled his drunk father into the water and held the son-of-a-bitch there for nearly three minutes, until he stopped struggling, and then Ergeny had swum underwater all the way around to the other side of the formation where he came up in the middle of a group of French tourists. He'd been underwater more than four minutes. He was already using his charms on the twenty-something blond tourist when somebody screamed that there was a body floating next to the rocks on the other side of the breakwater.

There'd been police and ambulances, even psychologists for the tourists who'd been traumatized by the tragic death so near their hotel. One of them even tried to help Ergeny through his obvious shock. He'd told her she was probably right – once it all sunk in, he'd probably cry.

As he slipped into the water, Ergeny wondered when it would sink in.

He remembered like it was yesterday, how his father had stared at him in disbelief that day under the water. Ergeny had let him get as drunk as he'd wanted, even brought an extra bottle from the reserve under the sink, just for the occasion. He'd been diving since he was eight years old, with Miguel Enrique's father, Angel. Every day he practiced holding his breath, longer and longer. He timed himself with the old clock at Jose Mendoza that had a second hand. At first even two minutes seemed impossible, but the more he ran and swam and exercised, the easier it got. Two minutes was his first milestone, then up to three. He noticed his arms and chest getting bigger the more he ran and practiced, and by the time he was twelve he hit four minutes for the first time, pumping his fists in the air and startling the teacher. By thirteen he'd improved to four and a half minutes, and on his fourteenth birthday, his mother had given him the mask and snorkel he used to this day. He'd gone to the ocean the next day and hatched his plan to make sure none of his brothers or sisters would have to deal with the terrors he had at the hands, and other parts, of their father. He knew, though, that he was already late. He'd heard his younger brother crying, and knew the look on his face and the way he was separating himself from everybody around him.

He knew his father wouldn't refuse a day of drinking at the beach. He'd have agreed to a day of drinking hanging upside down from his ankles. Just the two of them, this time, Ergeny had insisted. The others weren't good enough swimmers and he wanted to show him the new place he'd found to collect big lobsters.

Ergeny made some adjustments to his mask while he floated face-down on the surface. He cherished the first dive every time he came. This was when he would see the ocean in its purist sense, before his presence startled the colored fish and crawling creatures into their hiding places. He would often be able to scratch the back of a manta ray before it flapped its elegant wings and floated to another, less-occupied hunting spot. The first dive would tell him how successful his day would be. More of the big flat blue fish in the Batea meant less threat from barracudas or other predators. When there were quantities of sardines near the shore, normally it meant there were larger fish hunting nearby. Ergeny's mind calculated a mile-a-minute, like a computer, when he saw the first snapshot of his world below the water. He was like Diane Fossey with the apes, but his jungle was underwater. Here, in the calm under the surface, he felt safe and free. Nobody could do what he did here, and there was no one to judge him or tell him he had to keep secrets. He almost hated that he had to surface every few minutes – he'd have preferred to dive deeper and deeper, become one with the schools of fish that hardly scattered anymore when he passed through them. He speared fish he knew he could sell with ease, and never just for the sake of killing.

Sometimes, under the water, he felt the four-year-old inside of him return; the innocent kid who played with the stick and bottle cap, learning hand-eye coordination with the bigger kids on the street. Before his father came to him in the dark, touching Ergeny and making him touch him back, night after night. Secrets. Threats. Smell of alcohol too close. Pain. More threats. Shame. Bruises he had to lie about. Dirty little boy. Bad boy. Ugly boy.

He gulped the air into his snorkel. Today he would not go home to Theresa. She deserved better. And before Edith got to know him, it was better he left. He couldn't take the chance. Everyone told him he was just like his father, and he was afraid to find out if that was true. He loved his children – all of them – Sandra, Ergeny, Fidel and Edith, and even though he wouldn't want to, he would love the child Claudia carried inside her. He'd just never give any of them the chance to know the father he had.

He'd talk to Vilma the next day about setting up two more bank accounts.

A turtle caught his eye as it rounded an outcropping of coral to his left. There go my tires, he said to himself, and felt a twinge of pain from the gout as he flipped his fin to the side to push himself downward.

EDITH

Superman is Dead

Funerals in Cuba can be confusing, to say the least. If they're confusing for adults, imagine how they are for kids. Add to it the fact there was no body to watch over, and no one had actually confirmed he was dead.

Edith skipped between the rows of benches, where members of five families did their best not to stare at any of the others. Edith was going to be ten years old in two weeks, and her youngest half-brother, Michel Ernesto, was going on nine. They went to the same school, ate in the same cafeteria, and shared a bici-taxi home every day. They only lived half a dozen blocks from each other. Michel Ernesto lived in a fancy colonial house that had been made into a bed and breakfast hotel. Edith lived in a tiny wooden house that had been divided twice. It had only two rooms and a sort of a bathroom. She had a dark complexion, since her mother was black. Michel Ernesto had curly, almost blonde hair, like his mother Claudia.

Sandra was her oldest half-sister, and tended to her twin boys outside of the funeral hall, under the shade of the terrace. Aldo and Ariel were two years old, now, and kept Sandra busy. Nobody knew who the father was, and she didn't seem to care to share the information. She lived in the same house on Mercedes Street with her mother and half-brother, Leonardito. He was older than Edith and Michel Ernesto, but Sandra always insisted he share his toys with them when she took him to visit, which was not very often. Since the boys were born, she hadn't been over to visit once. Sandra was thirty-something, already, and Ergeny was in his late twenties. He had used the money he discovered on his twenty-first birthday to buy a plot of land down the coast from the Captain's place, only a couple of kilometers from the Batea. There were already a few flecks of grey in his close-cropped hair, but he was still strong and far too handsome for his own good. He seemed content, though, with his second wife, with whom he had two beautiful little girls, Marian and Ines, five and three. Fidel, for some reason, had remained single. No kids. No girlfriend. There was speculation that he was gay, but everybody assumed a guy was gay if he hadn't married by the time he was twenty. He was around twenty-five, now. His nest-egg had been used to upgrade his mother Maria's house with all of the things she could have wanted – starting with a new automatic washing machine and a big color television.

So all of the speculation about their father putting a bunch of money away for the big place on the beach, or a car, or any of a dozen things they'd heard over the years, had been proven wrong when each of his children turned twenty-one. One after another, Vilma, the bank manager, had advised each of them of the sum of money in their names.   Sandra was first, and still most people thought she was the only one, being his first child. When Ergeny received a visit on his birthday, he was probably more surprised than anyone. He'd had less contact with his father than any of his half-brothers and –sisters. The sum was almost the same – enough to get started in any type of business he wanted, or to buy a reasonable house. Ergeny had his own house by seventeen years old, so the land out by the ocean was within his reach after he included his house in the deal. He was happy there, with the most basic house, surrounded by chickens and pigs and goats. He looked like a Hollywood movie star, tanned as dark as his little half-sister Edith. Fidel had kept to himself as he'd grown older, choosing to lead tourists on dives out on the coral reefs. He taught diving at the all-inclusive hotels, and could speak enough of English, German and French to get along without any trouble. He'd heard every joke about his name so many times, and in so many languages, that he had a quick-witted answer for all of them. He brought his tips home and handed them all to his mother, Maria, and spent his free time teaching his cousin Miguel Enrique's kids to swim and dive and speak a little of each language.

Little Michel Ernesto was the only question mark in the group, now.   Ergeny had never married his mother, Claudia. He'd gone fishing the night he learned she was pregnant, and just never came home. Like Elvis, he was spotted plenty, but never really confirmed. He'd spent some time in Havana, with some cousins on his mother's side. Then there was a rumor he'd settled in Playa Santa Maria, a beautiful resort area on the north coast of Cuba. In Cayo Coco, another group of all-inclusive hotels further down the island, on the famous keys, he'd taken up lobster diving again. They'd even sent home reports he'd been spotted in Santiago. The only person who had any steady contact with him was Vilma, from the bank. He sent the money back to her without fail, to be divided equally between his children. Claudia's aunt had indeed left everything to her when she'd passed a few years earlier, and besides the beautiful house full of antiques, there'd been a sizable bank account by Cuban standards. Claudia and Michel Ernesto would not lack anything they needed. Vilma shook her head when she divided the money into equal piles, every month. It hadn't mattered one bit to Ergeny that his youngest son would have more money than all of the rest of the family together. He was still blood, and got the same treatment.

Edith kissed Sandra on the cheek, and waited for each of the twins to give her a slobbery kiss on hers. She was the little mother hen to all of the children. She loved Sandra most, though. Sandra was nearly the same age as her own mother, and always treated her special. She invited her to watch all of the latest animated movies on the DVD player she'd bought with her 'Daddy Money' as Edith called it. She was already making plans for her own treasure, and she still had more than eleven years to wait. She'd spent it so many times over in her mind. At first, when she learned of the money that awaited her, she was going to buy a castle with fairies and princes and winged horses. By eight years old, she already had her eyes on the Hotel Trinidad del Mar, sure she could buy it and make it into her own private playground. Now that she was a mature almost-ten-year-old, she was much more pragmatic. A new kitchen for her mother, and roller blades for her.

The funeral hall was bursting with people who wanted to pay their final respects to Ergeny. Obviously, with five separate families, all of whom sent a dozen or so representatives, it kept the ladies in the kitchen busy just making coffee for the relatives. Every restaurant, bed and breakfast and hotel in the city had one or two attendees. Ergeny'd single-handedly supplied most of the lobster and specialty fish all of them had served until the day he left. Luckily for all of them, Ergeny Junior had been prepared to take his place. Vilma and half of the bank staff were there from the first moment the doors opened. She'd watched him grow up on the streets of the Barranca, and she was one of the very few people alive who had an inkling of what had gone on behind the old wooden doors of the house on the corner. Her husband was a drinker, like Ergeny's father, and she'd heard a few things she wished she hadn't. It had been her honor, she said, to have helped Ergeny with his plan to take care of each of his children. She alone had seen the tears he shed when he made her promise to take care of the money. She was also the only person he told of his plan to go to the United States via Ecuador. She'd begged him to change his mind, but he'd told her that his mind had been made up. There was nothing left in Cuba for him. He wanted to start over and hoped to send much more money to his kids once he got to the land of opportunity.

Sandra had sent Leonardito over to the little shop across the street from the funeral hall with enough money to buy some sweets for each of the kids under ten. She knew they'd all be going home soon. The twenty-four hour vigil was reserved for the older family. Friends and acquaintances filtered in and out all day long. News travelled fast in the small city, and everybody knew Ergeny, for better or worse. Even Chichi, the bicycle bandit, as he'd been known, made a special point of driving into town in his red convertible that he rented out for fifteenth birthday parties now that he'd retired to his beach house. Joseito had long-since succumbed to the cancer. Sandra's grandfather, who sold flowers across the street from the cemetery, sent half a dozen beautiful arrangements to brighten up the dull surroundings. All there had been where the casket normally stood was a big picture of that million-dollar smiling face.

Sandra had cried off and on all day, usually when one of her half-brothers and -sisters arrived. They shared something, even if that something was an absent father. She really felt like their big sister, and kept an eye and ear out for any tidbit she might learn. She'd been at the hospital for the births of Ergeny's two daughters, and his wife had spent a week helping her after the twins were born prematurely, and she'd had to stay at the hospital in Sancti Spiritus. Edith's mother, Theresa, had even lent her a room in an aunt's house who lived near the hospital.

It was probably true that each of Ergeny's wives resented the next one in line, because there was almost always an overlap. He was never, ever without a woman, until the day he left Trinidad. Dalila, Sandra's mother, must have hated Lillet, Ergeny's, and she would have wanted to strangle Maria, Fidel's mom. So it would have been that Maria would have blamed Theresa for the break-up of their marriage, even though he'd been living alone for several years before he met Theresa. He had still been technically married to Maria; and Theresa would have assumed that Claudia, who had been her school friend, had betrayed her, hoping to snag Ergeny. The truth was something more complicated. The five women just knew they had been a part of a complicated man's life. Each wife, after Dalila, would have heard him crying into his pillow before he drifted off to sleep.

Sandra caught Theresa's eye. They were the closest in age. Theresa had been a very good woman, and the fact that she never married again, or even dated another man, was testament to her strong faith and the love she had felt for Sandra's father. She had dedicated her life to Edith, and from what Sandra saw at school when she checked on her siblings, she was a fine student, and always impeccably clean and with her hair perfectly braided. Edith was blessed, or cursed, with her father's smile. She wondered what trouble it would cause her kid sister in the future.

Leonardito returned with the treats, and one by one the mothers gathered their flocks to get them home before dark. Edith made her rounds again, giving each of her extended family a kiss on the cheek. So far beyond her years, Edith pleaded with her mother to let her stay longer, but she lost the battle. Theresa shared a glance with Sandra, and she nodded her approval at her leaving with the child. Sandra's boys had gone home with their grandmother hours earlier.

As darkness encroached on the funeral parlor, another round of bitter coffee was served by the couple that attended every death. They looked like zombies – walking around with their big round trays, filled with tiny plastic cups of coffee provided by the state. Almost everyone took one, though, no matter how awful it tasted. Drinking the little espressos was just what you did, in Cuba. Conversations inevitably turned to the weather – it had been unusually hot this year, which had affected the avocados, and the price had soared. The mangos seemed to have fared better; every corner had mangos of every type, and there were dozens of different mangos in Cuba, each with a distinct flavor -- one was better for juice, and another for eating right from the tree.

Edith hummed a song she liked on the way home. It was a long walk to the Barranca, and her feet already hurt from the too-small church shoes she wore for the occasion. Theresa admonished her for singing, considering her father was not yet in the ground. Music would not be heard for months, out of respect.

"But they aren't going to put him in the ground, anyway," she reasoned.

"Don't disrespect your father!" came the abrupt reply.

"I'm not disrespecting him. My daddy's not dead, anyway." Edith hadn't cried at all from the news about her father they'd received less than twenty four hours earlier. She'd shown almost no emotion at all.

Theresa stopped in her tracks, under the dim light from one of the few street lights that still had a bulb. "Young lady, where do you get such ideas?"

"If they didn't find his body, then I don't believe he's dead."

Edith curtsied, and offered her hand to an invisible prince. She had more imaginary friends than real ones, it seemed.

"Sometimes I feel like smacking your imagination right out of your head, Edith. It's hard enough to deal with all of this without you talking crazy like that."

Edith winced from the pain in her feet. "Can I take my shoes off, Mom?"

Theresa looked around, hoping to see a bici-taxi prowling nearby. "If you think your feet'll hurt less barefoot, go ahead, but take your stockings off before you touch the dirt." There was no one on the street but the dirty old garbage truck, making its rounds, puffing more black smoke out of the broken exhaust than the actual garbage it picked up. The sidewalk was reasonably clean, though, so Edith held her shoes by two fingers and skipped along ahead, while Theresa kept vigil. It was a small city, so there wasn't a single block that she didn't know one or more of the families. Nobody knew any of the street names, anymore. After the revolution, the "party" had changed all of the names to better suit the cause, and the names that had been there for more than four hundred years were replaced by heroes of the revolution.

If anyone asked directions in Trinidad, they were given instructions by the better-known people, not by street names and numbers. "You're looking for Pepe the carpenter? Oh, that's easy – at the little v-shaped park, take the street that goes to the hospital, then turn not at the first right, but the second. There's the doctor's place; you know, the doctor with the limp? Go down the block about halfway, and Pepe lives in front of the house where the Yuma and the candongera Marla just moved in." In this way, you could find anybody you wanted to. The tradesmen were usually the best references – everybody needed a plumber or an electrician or a carpenter sometime, so they knew where most of them lived. Everyone else was located in relation to them, or a specific house that was known to everyone. "You know the big yellow house that the roof caved in two years ago in the hurricane? She lives four houses down from there."

Theresa could hear the music from the novela coming from almost every house she passed. The evening soap operas from Mexico or Brazil or Colombia were a religion in Cuba. Nobody missed them. Who didn't like to see how the rich people lived with their fancy houses and perfect hair and makeup, and the clothes and shoes? There were also Cuban soap operas, and for some reason, there was always plenty of food in the refrigerators and nobody wore the same clothes twice. The lady of the house never had a mop in her hand, splashing water on the floors, and the patios never had old wire strung every which way to hold the drying laundry. Their only problems seemed to be they didn't know who their real father was, and the perfect and wealthy landowner's daughter was in love with the wrong man. Tonight was the Mexican novella, with Sebastian Ruly. That man was a dream, no doubt about it. Theresa smiled when she thought about how he always had some reason to be peeling off his shirt, and her heart skipped a beat, every time. His chest and stomach reminded her of Ergeny's, back when she'd first seen him at her grandmother's house one night when they were performing a Santera cleansing ceremony. Ergeny could have been a star in any novela, with his shockingly good looks and perfect body. Theresa was nearly thirty, now. Where had the time gone? Where had her life gone?

Edith had stopped a few houses ahead and was peeking in the window at a color television. Theresa picked up her pace.

"Get off of that veranda this minute! Don't you have any manners?"

"But this is the part where they drugged Sebastian and held him in the shack."

"We'll see the end of it by the time we get home," Theresa assured her, trying to keep her voice near a whisper so as not to draw the attention of the owner of the house. She was black, and her daughter was mulata, and that was enough for the whiter folks to assume they were casing the house to send someone back to steal something later.

"But I want to see what happened to my daddy!"

Theresa had arrived at the house by now, and signaled with her eyes and the purse of her lips for Edith to get moving, NOW. Edith knew that look, and didn't wait for the next phase, which involved twisting of braids, something she avoided whenever possible.

When they had gotten out of earshot of any houses, Theresa stopped Edith and grabbed her shoulder and turned her to face her mother. "I'll tell you what happened to your father when we get home, young lady, and not before. And trust me, it's not a novela."

Edith knew her mother was upset, because she never laid a hand on her. She was almost ten years old, and already knew when it came to her father, there was no fooling around. Her mother never stopped loving him, and by the looks of it, she had no plans to stop anytime soon.

She decided to keep her comments to herself, the rest of the way home. It was a long walk, and her feet were getting sore from the cobble stones whenever she had to cross a street, and many of the sidewalks were cracked and uneven. She knew better than to complain, though. Her mother was in one of her moods, and she'd seen tears when they passed under the rare street lamps that gave off any light. For some reason, Theresa took a different route home than they had taken when the bici-taxi had taken them to the funeral hall earlier in the day. She turned and followed the street that during the day was filled with hundreds of stalls in the Candonga, where her sister Sandra still worked every day. Edith had other family members who sold wooden figures in the Candonga, and many others who chose to sell their handmade crafts wholesale to the venders. It was hard to make a living as a wholesaler, but some people didn't like the idea of selling to the Yumas all day long, and having so many people say no. Selling was a hard job, too. The difference was the wholesalers might sell a wooden carving that took them half a day to make for a dollar to the venders, and the venders would sell them for five dollars, or even ten. It was the same with the crocheted clothing. A good salesperson like Sandra couldn't keep up crocheting everything for herself. She could sometimes sell ten sweaters or little girls' dresses in a day, and even though she was fast, she couldn't crochet more than one piece in a night, and especially now with the twins to take care of. Sandra had a group of women that kept her stall supplied, and she sent back anything that didn't meet her strict standards.

Edith blew a kiss to Sandra's area, which was nothing more than a few bolts sticking out of the cobblestones where she anchored her home-made stall of re-bar and fishnet. Somehow she found a way to make it look just a little better than the other fifty stalls that sold the exact same product.

Edith laughed to herself when she remembered the time when one of the competitive crochet sales ladies had tried to change Sandra's "luck". She'd arrived one morning to find four broken eggs – one at each corner of her stall, and some sort of Santeria powder spread all around in the center. That was the day a Yuma came to her stall and bought nearly everything she had. Sandra had shouted at the top of her lungs, "Could the person who left the powder in my stall please do it every day?" There was never powder in her stall again.

The streets around the Candonga still confused Edith – there were lots of short streets at strange angles, and she'd been lost before when she'd walked home with friends and had to double back to familiar routes. Her mother, though, knew every street in Trinidad, although she couldn't remember the new names. Her family had been in Trinidad since the slave trade, and the black families were generally larger than the white, or even the mulatos, like Edith. Her ancestors had settled on the outskirts of the town, at the time, where the slaves had been delegated after they were freed, and that area had eventually been overtaken by the growth of the colonial city. Now the Barranca was just one more neighborhood in the city. There just happened to be a much higher prevalence of colored families there.

When they emerged from a street Edith had never set foot on, she was surprised to discover they were only a block from the one they lived on, and even closer to her grandmother's house. She made a mental note to remember this street in the future. She took a snapshot with her brain – the CDR was on one side of the street – Committee for the Defense of the Revolution – she had to learn about them in pre-school. On the other side was the little shop where the quota was dispersed for her family. A few kilos of dirty rice, beans that were more stones than beans, and some dark sugar and coffee mixed with grain, and as they say in Cuba, "Stop counting!"

Her bladder reminded her she was almost home. She never used a bathroom anywhere but in her own house, mostly because there were very few public bathrooms for Cubans, but more because most bathrooms in Cuba were not cleaned regularly, and seldom had water or light bulbs in them. The watered-down orange drink they'd given the kids at the funeral hall wanted out, and now.

Theresa fumbled with the key in the ancient lock, and scraped the giant door along the floor. She needed to get someone to reset the old forged-steel hinges so the door didn't drag. She didn't want to damage the old wood any more than it already was. She'd heard of Yumas paying two hundred dollars for an old colonial door so they could make them into tables and other furniture. The first person who showed her two hundred dollars, she'd have the door off the hinges in thirty seconds flat, and would buy a new aluminum one that would open and close properly.

Edith was inside and into the bathroom faster than the cockroaches could scurry into the cracks in the walls. Theresa went straight to her kitchen, as was her habit, to make sure the clean dishes were still clean and everything was as she'd left it. Something she spotted hit a nerve, reminding her of Ergeny, and she had to support herself with both arms against the cement counter. Edith rounded the corner and saw her mother crying again, and decided it was a good time to change into her night clothes, hanging the dress carefully on her one and only plastic hanger. All the rest were twisted pieces of wire, and the rust sometimes stained her white clothes. Her prettiest dress would never touch one of the metal hangers. She wiped her shoes clean and set them in their space in the closet where her three pairs of shoes were kept – one pair for school, one to play, and these ones for special occasions. There had been very few special occasions, unfortunately, and she was already outgrowing them, even though they were like new. They had been handed down to her from a cousin, and there would be another owner soon enough. Hopefully her cousin had outgrown her new shoes by now, because they were beautiful!

Theresa had gathered herself and followed Edith's lead and hung her own dress on another plastic hanger. She slipped into her nightgown as well, all the while not saying a word.

Edith folded the colorful bedspread back onto itself, and then again, as her mother had shown her to do by the time she was four years old. She hung it carefully over the back of the wicker kitchen chair. The wicker from the bottom of the chair had been replaced with a piece of plywood that had been discarded. She was nervous, wondering if her mother had forgotten what she'd told her on the street. She knew they needed to sleep early, so they could be back in time for the ceremony in the morning. They would normally form a procession to the cemetery, where the casket would be lowered into the family plot and sealed with concrete by the workers there. She'd been allowed to go to the cemetery the previous year when her paternal grandfather had passed. Edith had been his adoration, and her mother thought it might help her grieving process to see where his body was laid to rest. For her father, though, without a body to carry to the plot, they had decided to have a small ceremony for the family, or in this case, the families, at the Batea, Ergeny's favorite diving site. A bus had been arranged to pick everyone up at the street that led to La Boca, across the tracks. That was one of the most common meeting points in Trinidad, where the largest new neighborhood, the Purisima, was located. The bus would be there promptly at nine, the driver had said, so they could count on it not arriving before nine-thirty. 'Promptly' in Cuba was a sort of estimate, but there were always factors that caused it to spread into 'mas o menos', more or less.

Edith had her own little bed next to her mother's, but it was used more as a staging area for the laundry to be folded than anything else. Her mother preferred to have her sleep in the same bed with her, and she didn't know how she would ever fall asleep if her mother didn't scratch her back and give her little butterfly kisses on the back of her head. She always tucked her two dolls into the small bed, and always on their sides, with one scratching the other's back. Her mother always woke up earlier than she did – another habit from when her father lived with them – and rearranged the dolls so they appeared to be awake and ready for a new day. She'd asked her mother why she had never had more children, and her reply was four brothers and sisters should be enough for anyone. The truth was, she could never feel the same for another man as she had for Edith's father.

"Sweetheart," Theresa whispered, breaking the long silence, handing her a glass of milk she had warmed on the hotplate. "Drink your milk and brush your teeth and come to bed. I want to tell you about your father and what happened."

Edith drank her milk faster than usual, remembering at the last second not to wipe her milk mustache with the back of her hand. The government toothpaste was terrible, but they had other priorities for the dollar that the good stuff cost in the TRD store. She swished it between her teeth, trying to get the most out of the watery, tasteless paste. When she visited her half-brother Michel Ernesto, she always brought her toothbrush with her to take advantage of the delicious mint toothpaste they had. If she could, she'd shower there, too, with the hot water. They had a big cistern, and even a pressure system in their house, and he told her she could shower for as long as she wanted. At home, the few drops that came from the gravity-fed, rusty pipes were hardly enough to make any suds with the dried-up soaps they had. Her mother spent her hard-earned money, though, to buy the best shampoo she could, and every Tuesday and Saturday she would wash and brush Edith's hair and braid it in a new design every time. Where she'd learned so many types of braids, Edith had no idea. She kicked off her house slippers and was under the snow white sheet in one move.

"You know I loved your father, right?" It seemed an odd way to start, being as there was nothing more obvious in the world. Her mother had already dedicated more than ten years of her life to a man who left her after two years with a baby to care for.

"Yes, Mother, I know."

"So what I'm going to tell you isn't easy for me to tell, or for you to hear." Theresa looked

Edith directly in the eyes. "Do you really want to me to tell you?"

This was going to be a grown-up talk, Edith knew, and for some reason she felt her eyes welling up with tears. Her father was Superman and Batman and Spiderman and every other hero to her, off saving the planet from untold horrors. She could only nod, holding her mother's gaze.

"Where do I start? Your father was very troubled about things from his past, things he never talked to anybody about."

"What kind of things?" Edith had never heard about anything bad in her father's past.

"Things that children shouldn't ever even have to know about, let alone experience. I figured it out because I'd seen the same symptoms when I was younger, with a little girl who lived near my grandmother. We walked past her house just a few minutes ago on our way home. That's why I made the detour, because I'd been thinking about her since…"

Edith was old enough to imagine what her mother was hinting at – things she'd been warned about time after time – not to sit on strange men's laps, don't let anybody touch your private parts. She shivered involuntarily at the very idea.

"Is that why Daddy left?"

"That, and a whole lot of other reasons, I'm sure. But one thing's certain – he didn't leave because of you, or because he didn't love you very much. Just the opposite, I'm sure."

Her mother had always told Edith her father loved her and he'd left because he truly thought it was best for her and her mother, but somehow hearing it at that moment was different, more important, considering he was gone forever, now. She felt two big tears escape from her eyes, and didn't try to stop them or even wipe her cheeks. Her father deserved her tears.

"So, you've heard all of the stories about how he moved from place to place, never really settling down anywhere?"

Edith nodded. She'd colored little hearts on all of the places in Cuba she'd heard he'd been. The little map looked like it would be covered completely by hearts any time.

"About a year ago, Chichi came to the house, asking about some papers Ergeny said he needed."

Edith thought it sounded strange to hear her mother use her dad's first name out loud. She had always referred to him as 'your father' or 'daddy'.

"There was only one reason for him to need copies of his birth certificate and the other papers he kept in the plastic bag above the closet – he had decided to leave Cuba."

"That's when he went to Colombia, right?" Edith had overheard bits of conversations over the last few days, and knew her dad had been in Colombia when he died.

"Well, not exactly. You know it's difficult for us Cubans to travel outside of the country." Edith nodded, blinking back more tears. "A lot of Cubans have started to go to Ecuador, where they don't need a visa, or an invitation letter. Your father got mixed up with a group of men who made a plan to go to Ecuador, and through a person one of them knew of, sneak across the border into Colombia, where they would fly to Mexico and then find their way to the American border, where they could enter the US as Cubans, and start a new life, there."

"So Daddy was in Ecuador, first?" She wasn't sure where Ecuador, or Colombia were, but she would find them in the old atlas at school.

"Yes, he arrived in Ecuador about two weeks ago, and even visited some friends from Trinidad who live there. They're the ones who got word back to his brother here that he'd gone with the other guys to meet up with the person who would cross them into Colombia in his van."

Edith tried to form a mental picture of the other men, but mostly cartoon characters popped into her head. One of them was Pop-eye, the sailor man; another was el Chavo del ocho. Her father

130

was the most handsome of all of them, she was sure of that.

"It turned out this man was a very bad person. He tricked your father and the others into trusting him. He made them hand over their passports and other documents and all of their money, 'for safe keeping', and had them write down a list of contacts in Cuba in case anything happened to them, so he could do them a favor and advise them. Then they crossed the border into Colombia at a point where he knew the guards and immigration people."

"How did you learn about that?" Edith wanted to know everything.

"One of the men came to Trinidad a few days ago, with your father's barracuda-tooth chain, and found Ergeny."

Edith snuggled in a little closer to her mother. The bad part was coming soon – she could feel it.

"Shortly after crossing the border, the van was attacked by masked men carrying big guns and shouting to them to go into the jungle. The driver made a big show about being surprised and supposedly gave the men all of the money in the bag, with all of the documents, and they let him go with his van. It was obvious to everyone they'd planned it all along."

"Were there lions and tigers in the jungle?" Tarzan appeared in her mind, swinging from vine to vine.

"No, Honey, in that jungle there aren't any lions or tigers. Unfortunately, there are much worse dangers, like evil men with guns and no conscience."

She didn't want to interrupt to ask what conscience meant, so she just let her mother continue. She hoped she'd understand as she went on.

"There's a group of bad men in Colombia they call FARC – they kidnap and kill people for money, and for political reasons, because they don't like the government there."

Edith knew about people not liking the government. She'd heard her cousin Miguel Enrique say lots of bad things about Fidel and Raul and the Cuban government, but somebody always 'shhhed' him so the neighbors didn't overhear. Miguel Enrique had joined a group that was trying to change the system in Cuba, whatever that was.

"They stripped your father and the others to their underwear, and made them march in circles for hours until they were exhausted and disoriented. Then the bad men drank cool water and spit it on the ground, but didn't let their captives have even a sip."

Edith hated these men already. She thought about her dad, in a jungle, sweating, and not being able to drink water.

"They did the same thing for three days. No food, no water, while the FARC men drank and ate in front of them."

Now Edith cried even harder, curling herself into a fetal position on the bed.

"I think that's enough for tonight, Sweetheart." Theresa's emotion was at seeing her daughter suffer.

"No, Mom, please... I want to know... I need to know."

"They started to threaten to kill them if they didn't pay more money. Of course, none of them had any money left after the driver had given up all of their belongings earlier."

"So what did they do?"

"That's when it became clear the driver had been one of them – they pulled out the list of contacts, and shoved it into their faces." Theresa searched her daughter's eyes for understanding. As if she was calculating something in her head, she made the connection and nodded. "They had no cellular service in the jungle, so they threw the men into a truck and drove out to a highway, about an hour from where they had been held.

Still no water or food, and the men were getting weak."

"My Daddy would have been the strongest," interjected Edith.

"I'm sure he was. Your father was very strong." She saw the reaction to the past tense, and paused for a minute.

Edith gave her a look that asked for more.

"I guess they drove to an old bridge over a river," Theresa continued, feeling like she needed to get it over with sooner than later. "A very high bridge. There were armed men on each end of the bridge, and they parked in the middle. The leader took out his cell phone and pushed it into the first guy's hands. 'Call home. You've got two phone calls to get a thousand dollars, or I'll be making the third call with the news.'" Theresa saw the look of horror on her daughter's face, and superimposed it onto Ergeny's face, as he must have looked there on the bridge. "The first call didn't go through, but the second one connected to his father in Camaguay. He knew his father didn't have a thousand, or even a hundred dollars. He'd given him every penny he had already for the trip to the United States."

"What happened to the man, then?"

Theresa swallowed, deciding if she should tell Edith the truth, knowing it was a too much for the average ten-year-old, but also knowing Edith wasn't the average.

"Honey, this is hard to hear – they pushed him to the edge of the bridge and shot him and let him fall into the river a hundred feet below. They made your father and the other men watch."

Edith made an involuntary sniffle, sort of a half-breath that caught in her throat. This couldn't be how her superhero daddy died, too.

"The man who came to Trinidad to find Ergeny was luckier. He had a connection to family in Miami, and after what they'd just seen, he made no mistakes. The relative in Miami assured him they were depositing the thousand dollars at Western Union within the hour."

Edith brightened. She knew her dad could get money. She knew about the bank accounts for his children, and how there was already a lot of money in her own. She breathed a sigh of relief. Her father would not have been shot on the bridge.

"The next guy was from Havana, and it took three phone calls to pool enough money to keep him alive, but it couldn't be deposited until the banks opened on Monday, and it was a Saturday evening when they called from the bridge."

"So they didn't shoot him, right?"

"No," she continued. "They made him sit on the edge of the bridge, facing away from the others. They told him to get comfortable, because he'd be there until the money arrived."

"And what happened to my dad? He gave them the money, right?"

Theresa hardly knew how to begin. She knew Edith knew about the money in the bank nobody could touch until she turned twenty-one. She also knew Sandra and Ergeny and Fidel had already received their windfalls of cash, and any one of them would have paid the ransom without hesitation.

"Your father hadn't marked down any contacts on the paper except his cousin who lived in Mexico. They passed the phone to him, and Ergeny just told him to tell his children he loved them."

Edith looked at her mother as though she must have been making it up.

"Apparently, after he hung up, they called the family back in Miami, and they confirmed the deposit of $1,000.00. Probably as a signal to the rest, they threw him a pair of pants and told him he was free to go."

Edith perked up at the thought that the kidnappers had hearts somewhere, deep down.

"So my father knew to pay them, too, right?"

Theresa wanted to lie to her daughter, tell her anything but the truth, but she knew too well one lie led to another and another, and it would never end. "Honey, the man told your brother he felt a need to hug each of the other captives, and when he got to him, your father pulled off his tooth chain and told him to get it back to his daughter, Sandra."

Edith had seen Sandra, just hours earlier, with the chain in her hands, running her fingers over the teeth like they were some sort of rosary.

"Why didn't my father call us to send the money? I don't understand."

"Sweetheart, there are a lot of people who have tried to understand the reasons your father has done a lot of things in his life, but none of us ever understood him. All you can do is accept that he did what he thought was right, and what was right for his children. He hadn't worked hard all his life to give everything back to a bunch of criminals... that's what we assume, anyway."

Edith knew they were getting to the part she didn't want to hear, but something told her she needed to hear it – get it over with. She hesitated, fumbled over the words, "What happened after that?"

"The man said he didn't want to leave the others, but they insisted he go and tell their families. He passed the guards at the end of the bridge, and decided to go down to the river to get back to the main road from there. He told Ergeny he'd just gotten down to the edge of the water when he heard loud screaming and a commotion from above. There was a gun shot and he turned just in time to see two bodies falling into the river. He ran over and was able to pull out one of them.

Theresa paused, partly because she knew Edith was hearing something too horrible for a ten-year-old, and partly because she needed to take a breath, herself, before continuing.

Edith looked back at her, as if asking why she'd let this happen to her father.

"It wasn't your father he pulled out. It was the other man, from Bayamo. He'd been shot in the head."

Edith grasped at straws. "You said there was only one shot."

Theresa stroked a stray hair that had escaped from Edith's braids and pushed it behind her ear. "He only heard one shot, Edith. That doesn't mean there weren't more."

Edith stared at the ceiling, following the ancient wooden beams that had been patched with scabs of plywood and bolts after the last hurricane had cracked the main beam and the entire roof had almost come down on them. It still creaked when there was a strong wind, and sometimes her mother even moved the bed into the kitchen to sleep 'so we don't end up on top of the roof instead of under it, she'd say'.

"How far is a hundred feet?" she finally managed to ask.

Theresa could hear the wheels turning in her daughter's mind. "It's a long, long way," she managed, "like the tallest buildings in Havana. Remember when we were there two years ago? Remember the hotel Havana Libre, where we went up to the restaurant on the top to see the lights of the city?"

Edith remembered it well. It was her one and only visit to the capital, and she could recount every moment in detail, especially walking on the sea wall and watching the waves crash over it. She remembered how the cars looked smaller from the restaurant. She nodded her head to confirm she remembered.

"The man said he searched for hours for your father, but assumed he hadn't yet surfaced from the fall. Finally, afraid they'd come back and find him there, he decided to find his way back to Ecuador and come back to Cuba. He said it took him three days to get back to the airport, and he'd had to steal vegetables and fruit from gardens to survive."

Edith hadn't heard the last part, and didn't really care what the man had had to do. Her brain was still processing her father falling from the top of the Havana Libre hotel into the water. She imagined the pain of the impact, and hoped he hadn't suffered too much, especially under the water. She hardly remembered her father, but she imagined he hadn't changed from the picture he left in the entry with the giant barracuda and Sandra. He could beat a giant fish with three-inch-long teeth, but he couldn't beat evil men with guns.

"Mom, I think I don't want to hear any more about it," Edith said, barely a whisper. "Do you think we could say a prayer for Daddy, before we go to sleep?"

Theresa could only nod, the lump in her throat too big to let any words pass at the moment. She got up and found two candles, and carefully lowered the framed picture from the wall. "Let's make a little bit of an altar for your father, like we have for your grandpa." She pushed a small table into a corner of the bedroom, under the only window, and lit her candle, offering it to Edith to light the second one with. She was going to make a fresh pot of coffee, to place with the candles, as was the custom in Cuba, but changed her mind. "Your father hated coffee. Let's make him a sandwich from tomatoes and avocados, just the way he liked them, and a big glass of water."

Edith found a little smile and wiped her eyes again. "I'll get the water." Her mother sliced the loaf of crusty bread, and found the reddest tomato and the perfect avocado. It was truly an act of love, making the man a sandwich again after nearly ten years, just as she had the last morning he had left and never returned. She stopped before she closed it, and squeezed her eyelids between her thumb and forefinger. Three long breaths in and out, and she could finally straighten herself and close the sandwich, which she placed on the only plate left from her great-grandmother's gift for her fifteenth birthday. Four plates, four cups and saucers, and four bowls. The edges had little flowers hand-painted onto them. One by one, year by year, pieces had tumbled from someone's hands, or just cracked and broke with age. The cups and saucers were still intact, only because they were large tea cups, not the little ones used for coffee in Cuba. Two bowls remained, and this plate. She'd served Ergeny his first meal as her husband on one of these plates, and he'd smiled that amazing smile that said he'd liked the plain rice and brown beans and fried bananas.

Edith filled the glass up to the top with cool water they kept in a big jug in the refrigerator. She walked carefully, so as not to spill even a drop of her father's water. She nodded to her mother, who was finishing up the sandwich, letting her know she didn't need any help with this task. They placed the candles in little glasses Theresa had made from the bottom halves of two old soda bottles for the purpose. The sandwich plate took up most of the rest of the space on the tiny table. Edith placed the glass of water under her father's smiling image in the picture. Her mother got down on her knees in front of the table, and signaled to Edith to do the same. She was just about to kneel down when something occurred to her.

"Wait, I forgot one thing," she announced, heading toward the kitchen again. Theresa had no idea what she could be looking for, and stood up, just in time to see Edith return with something in the palm of her hand, and a little spoon in the other. When she got close enough, Theresa saw what Edith had thought of.

"You always said he liked salt water better than anything else in the world, right?" Edith said, dumping the salt into the glass, and mixing it with the spoon.

"He'd appreciate that, Honey," Theresa said, allowing herself a bit of a laugh. "He always told me not to put salt on his food, because he had enough in his cavities for any meal."

Then the two of them kneeled together and prayed for a full five minutes, before Theresa touched Edith's shoulder and pointed to the bed.

Theresa scratched Edith's back until her breath came evenly, signaling she'd gone to sleep, and watched the little candles flicker in the darkness, giving a spark of life to Ergeny's face with each ebb and flow of the flames. She could swear he was smiling at the salt water in the glass in front of him. She didn't know when she'd finally drifted into sleep, but her internal alarm brought her to her feet at four a.m. Some habits died harder than...

She laid out another dress for Edith to wear, and wiped the little dust her shoes had accumulated on the walk home the evening before. She knew she should have let out the seams of the dress. It was already too tight for Edith, but she didn't want her to go in the same dress as the previous day. Cuban pride. She looked over at the sewing basket, and realized there was time to do at least a little adjustment, and knew it would take her mind off of Ergeny. Edith looked like a little female version of him, sleeping so peacefully in the bed. She glanced over at the sandwich on the little table, and thought it was fitting that she eat from the same loaf, and sliced off a two inch piece, leaving twice that much for Edith, with the 'boob' as they called the ends in Cuba. She spread a thin layer of cream cheese and three slices of tomato. She couldn't help but smile when she reached for the container of salt. How had she grown up so fast?

She ate in silence, popping the seams of Edith's dress with her tiny nail clipping scissors. She noted that the dress had been let out before by the previous owner, so there was precious little fabric left to do it again. She'd gain so little, it was hardly worth the effort, but hopefully it would help avoid an embarrassing accident if Edith moved the wrong way and the old seams gave out. Theresa looked over at her foot-pedal sewing machine, knowing it would take only a few minutes to run up and down the seam with it, but chose to sew it by hand so as not to disturb Edith. She had no reason to rush – the bici-taxi had been arranged for eight-thirty, to give them plenty of time to arrive at the meeting point before nine. In her mind, she went over the checklist – two bottles of frozen water, the old umbrella for the sun at the Batea, old tennis shoes for Edith to wear to walk on the sharp volcanic rock, flower petals to toss into the ocean -- she'd stop at Sandra's grandfather's place on the way. Not much else. She glanced over at the little shrine and noted how the wax had formed two little flat islands with only a discolored spot in the center where the wicks had finally sputtered and died. Her neighbor made candles, so she'd give the wax to her and a few pesos to turn it into two more. Before leaving, she decided, she'd check to see if there were any big candles available to provide a more respectable tribute. With all of the Santeria in Trinidad, there were always candles burning for one reason or another, and everyone she knew lit a candle to ask for protection or speedy recovery or safe return. Every request for help from beyond involved candles. Her neighbor had a thriving business at a few pesos apiece.

Satisfied with her handiwork, Theresa plugged in her twenty-year-old iron – one of the few things she'd owned pre-Ergeny. Her great-grandmother had handed it to her when she wasn't much older than Edith, after she was chosen to receive a new one as part of a stimulus where her husband worked in the cane fields. Not that she didn't appreciate the iron, but in the earlier years, when Russian money and products poured into Cuba like a tap stuck open, a year of hard work and holding up your end of the party guidelines – basically saying yes to everything the government said, no matter how mundane – got a choice of a television or a big Russian refrigerator or a bicycle. Twenty years ago, an iron was a good item to receive. Now, a good worker was lucky to get an extra bag of rice or beans, or a new machete to work even harder with.

Dresses ironed, dishes cleaned and in their places, floor swept, tears wiped, Theresa decided it was time to wake Edith and begin the preparations for the day. It only took the tiniest touch on her shoulder to wake her. Theresa couldn't help but notice the switch that went off in the instant between waking and remembering her father and the sadness glazing over her eyes. Edith never complained about waking up and getting ready – she was a morning person; that she got from her father. She would go from sleeping to singing in five seconds flat. Not today, of course.

Edith sat up and wiped her eyes, dragging the dried remnants of the tears from the night before out of the corners with her baby fingers. She yawned audibly and stretched her arms until they looked like they would separate from her shoulders. She surveyed the small place, noting the bread and tomato on the table, the burned-out candles, and on her little bed beside her, she saw the yellow dress. Her eyes told her mother she couldn't put that dress on, and Theresa silently responded, holding up the needle and thread. Edith smiled. Somebody surely had a better mother than she had, but she couldn't think of who it might be.

They arrived at Sandra's grandfather's flower market just in time to see the old man closing the latch on the gate, dressed in a pair of poorly-ironed trousers, a guayabera that she knew must have been from when he was a much younger man, and a nice Panama hat and walking cane. He had favored his right leg since she knew him. Theresa asked if there was still time to buy some rose petals, and he produced a large bag he had set aside for the purpose. He handed it to Edith, and looked as if he was going to walk the kilometer to the meeting area. When Theresa pointed to the seat beside her, and hauled Edith onto her lap, he didn't decline. She knew he'd always thought of Ergeny as the worst kind of person, having left his granddaughter for another woman, the way he had. Knowing as he did how Ergeny had repeated the process ad nausea, surely hadn't raised his opinion. Still, though, he was a man of class, and he attended out of his sense of what was correct and decent. He wasn't going for Ergeny, that much was clear, but for Sandra and Fidel.

Edith had already polished off all of what had melted from both bottles of water by the time the bus pulled up promptly at nine-forty-eight, just in time to wait for two stragglers they could see trying to put on a show of hurrying down the street parallel to the railroad tracks. They must have had their clocks set on Cuban time. Sandra, Ergeny and Fidel clearly had not slept – they were dressed the same way they had been when Edith and Theresa had left the hall the previous night. Sandra still had a smile and a warm hug for Edith and Michel Ernesto, who had been waiting with Claudia when they'd arrived. The five brothers and sisters were together for the second time in their lives, and both had occurred less than twelve hours apart. The five mothers separated themselves in a manner so as not to sit next to their chronological 'replacements'. The only exception was Claudia, who had long-since made amends with her school friend, Theresa; she sat in the row of seats opposite her so their children could be near each other.

Edith tried to see what Ergeny held in his lap, under a thick towel. She didn't want to be rude and ask out loud, because he hadn't offered to show her. She could see he and Fidel both had their fins and masks with them, so they planned to get into the water. Edith had broken the family mold, because she had no love of the salt water. On the contrary, her mother had to prod her to get her feet wet when they went to the beach. He was obviously keeping it as a surprise. She could hardly look at Ergeny – he looked so much like her father in the picture in her living room – and he always winked at her, which made her blush.

The road to the Batea passed through La Boca, and Edith always loved the beach houses there. They seemed to be spread further apart from one another, as though space there wasn't at such a premium as it had become in Trinidad. They continued through the little community, past the little food stands and the big old truck with the tank of home-brewed beer on the back – a line-up already at ten in the morning of men with their empty soda bottles and their Cuban pesos that looked more like old napkins they were so limp from use. The Captain's house was alone on the right-hand-side of the road, converted into a fancy bed and breakfast some years earlier. There was some commotion as they approached the entrance to Ergeny's ranch, to the left, about two kilometers past the Captain's House. Probably by design, it was impossible to see any buildings from the road – there was a long curve from the entrance, so all you could see were trees from the bus windows. Edith spotted a mother goat with two tiny kids banging their heads against her udder, trying to fill their little bellies. Ergeny wasn't in any mood to brag about his place, and nobody coaxed him to do so. Somebody asked if his wife and girls were at home, and he said they'd probably have walked to the Batea by then.

Edith counted the family on the bus, and got to thirty when she heard a collective gasp from the others – as they rose over the small rise in terrain, they got their first look at the Batea. The ocean was like a plate that day, and there were at least fifty fishing boats, all anchored in a semi-circle, facing the Batea. The small family ceremony idea hadn't gone over well with Ergeny's "other" family. All of the men who made their living from the ocean had grown up with the diver, and had heard about the family's idea to pay tribute there. A few of the fishermen had come ashore and had already prepared a roaring fire, with two large tubs of boiling water. Beside them, they had arranged rocks to hold another big flat pan, already loaded with fresh fillets of every type of fish. Bottles of rum were already at various stages of empty, or full, depending on each's attitude.

There was a chorus of "Oh my God's" from the group on the bus, and through the open windows they could hear the sound of the ocean and seagulls that had joined the party, already swooping to steal the discarded parts of the fish and lobster that were being prepared. As the air brakes snorted their arrival, one of the cooks turned around to wave at the new arrivals. It was none other than Chichi, and it appeared he was the one who had orchestrated the amplification of the event into a full-blown fiesta.

Fidel helped Ergeny to carry the surprise, grabbing two corners of the towel in his strong fist, as did Ergeny with the other two corners. In his other hand, Ergeny carried a sack of cement that appeared to be less than half-full. They'd given the younger siblings the task of carrying their masks and fins. Edith had already switched into her tennis shoes, and followed so close to Ergeny that she nearly bumped into him a couple of times as he found his footing with the heavy load. Michel Ernesto was dressed for the beach, with store-bought water shoes to protect his feet from the sharp rocks. Claudia wore an elegant sun dress, and had decided this was a good day to air out all of her gold jewelry. She had aged into a beautiful woman, probably helped by never having to worry about where her next meal would come from, as most Cubans did. More than one of the fishermen had stopped what he was doing to admire her curves and elegance. She ignored all of them. Her attention was on Michel Ernesto and his eagerness to get wet. Her shoes were definitely not made for lava rock, and she chose her path deliberately to save them. When she was as close to the Batea as she cared to be, she pulled a giant towel from her shoulder bag. Any other Cuban would have cut a towel like that into three or four pieces, but Claudia wasn't your average Cuban woman, by any means. Her hair was perfect, her makeup looked like it had been professionally applied, and she had actual sculptured nails. Even her toenails matched. She managed to find a comfortable spot on the towel, and adjusted her large hat so it blocked the morning sun, smudged sun-block onto Michel Ernesto's back and shoulders, and released him to the water. He dove into the Batea, wanting to be first in the water, and he would surely be the last to get out.

Chichi handed out mouth-watering minuta – fish that had been cut open and doused in flour and a few select spices – from the pile set off to the side of the flames to keep warm. Nobody would leave there hungry that day. Fidel shook Chichi's hand firmly as he and Ergeny passed by with their load, looking for a flat spot to set it down for the preparations. When they found a spot, they were relieved to give their biceps a rest.

It was Ergeny who broke up the party with the loud voice that only a pair of lungs like his could produce. "I'd like the five children and their mothers to gather around here for a moment. There's something Sandra and Fidel and I have prepared for today."

Michel Ernesto reluctantly agreed to come out of the water and join them. He knew he was different from the rest, never having known his father, but he was proud to be included, as was Claudia, who always felt like a bit of an odd-shaped branch in the family tree, as it were. Chichi played the part of a gentleman, and offered an elbow to each Claudia and Theresa, to help them manipulate their way to the gathering spot. Even though he was barefoot, he looked like he could have walked over sharp glass without noticing. His skin was so tanned from his life in the sun that there was little difference between his and Theresa's color.

Fidel had offered a hand to Sandra, but she was as sure-footed as the men, and needed no help.

Ergeny had turned his attention to the bag of cement, from which he pulled a plastic pail and a mixing stick. Inside the pail was a pre-mixed portion of cement and fine gravel, and one of the fishermen poured water from a big thermos into the pail.

"All of you know that our father was more comfortable below the surface than on top of it." Ergeny spoke loud enough for the small group to hear, and watched the nods of agreement from the family. "So there is some poetic justice to the fact that he left this world in the way he probably would have wanted. Fidel and Sandra and I had a chance to discuss how we'd like to pay our last tribute to our father, and we decided having his name on a headstone in the cemetery wasn't what he or we wanted. Fidel and his mother know some of the finest artisans in Trinidad, and they were kind enough to help us make something we think our father would be proud of."

With that said, Ergeny and Fidel pulled off the towel that covered the most amazing sculpture of a coral reef, including a diver, complete with snorkel and fins and a spear gun at the ready. Below was a flat spot where the words "Ergeny lived here" carved into it in perfect lettering. The 'd' had been crossed out roughly, and an 's' chipped into the space above, changing 'lived' to 'lives'. Behind the coral, there was a space left open of about ten by thirty inches, where the concrete Ergeny was mixing would obviously fill.

When he'd finished the mixture, Ergeny poured it into the space, while Fidel scraped the excess that had dripped over the edges. Between them, they made it as smooth as a glass table. Fidel tested the surface every few minutes while the family admired the spectacular work of the artist. The diver could have been Ergeny himself, with its muscular legs and barrel chest. Michel Ernesto touched the point of the spear and with the surprise on his face, confirmed it was indeed sharp enough to draw blood. Sandra was the one to point out that the spear had been made from a sharpened crochet hook, looking very much like the spear Ergeny used.

Fidel gave Ergeny a nod that the concrete was ready, and signaled with a gesture of his hand above the flat space that Sandra would be the first to leave her print. Sandra had been prepared, knowing what they were planning, and pushed her left hand deep enough into the mixture to leave a perfect print. Then, she slipped the barracuda tooth from the gold chain around her neck, and pressed it into the impression of her fingers, making it look like she was holding it in her hand. Ergeny went next, with his hand as close as possible to Sandra's, one finger overlapping her thumb print. Fidel took his lead, and did the same, keeping the chain intact. He called Edith over, and helped to push her small fingers and palm into the concrete next to his, and then did the same with little Michel Ernesto. When all of them had made their marks, there was just enough space left for Ergeny to scrawl the date into the surface.

Claudia was the only person who had brought a camera, probably because she was the only one who actually owned a camera. She asked the five children to gather together and put their hands into their respective marks, and took the first picture ever of Ergeny's five children together. It was Edith who suggested they do the same with the five mothers, and after some hesitation on some of their parts, their children convinced them to leave their emotions behind and do it for them. One by one, the ex-wives and Claudia found a position they could hold and put their hands over their children's imprints. In the background of the pictures, boats of every shape and color bobbed gently on the smooth surface of the ocean. Ergeny and Fidel sat next to each other, pulling on their dive suits and propping their masks and snorkels on their heads, ready to be pulled down into place. Each of them slipped into the water, and tossed their fins within reach. Chichi and another fisherman carefully passed the sculpture to them, and they balanced it on a natural ledge until they were ready. While the other held the sculpture, each prepared his mask and pulled it into place, and then slipped on their fins. A moment later, a thumbs up passed between them, and they lifted it from its perch and below the surface. The bottom was relatively flat, so they were able to get a firm grip on each side of the coral protrusions, and underwater it didn't weigh nearly as much, so they could hold it without as much effort as they moved away from the shore to the spot both of them knew so well. It was about forty meters from where they had entered – the spot where the natural reef really began, where the underwater life of the ocean was so active. The sculpture was modelled after the actual coral from this part of the ocean, so when they placed it onto the reef bed, it looked like it had grown from that very spot.

On the surface, all they could make out were two blurry figures moving out from the rocks, until they were lost from view altogether. For the mothers and other family, it seemed like an eternity had already passed since the two half-brothers had filled their lungs and submerged. In reality, it had barely been two minutes. Edith worried most of everybody. She didn't like the ocean at all. Michel Ernesto had jumped back in the water immediately after the pictures, and dove and surfaced every ten or fifteen seconds, trying to see more than the rest.

Ergeny gave Fidel another thumbs up, satisfied with the angle the monument had settled to, and Fidel grabbed his half-brother's hand like an arm-wrestler, and pulled him close and wrapped his left arm around his shoulder. They remained that way for a long moment, both proud of what they had done for their father.

Fidel, who had long-since traded the snorkel for an air tank, had to head for the surface first, and he motioned to Ergeny that he was on his way. Ergeny had plenty of air left in his lungs, and decided it was a good day to use it all. He watched Fidel break the surface above him and continue toward the group waiting for them.

Ergeny admired the monument as he began a slow backward movement, his large fins looking like a manta ray as he kicked his feet in rhythm to the song he sang to himself. Two large blue fish came from deeper water, and went straight to the new coral, as though doing a new-home inspection. Ergeny smiled in his mask, sending a string of bubbles to the surface.

"Looks like a good day, Dad... no barracudas in sight."

Edith decided it was as good a day as any to get her feet wet, and slipped her feet into the warm water as she watched Ergeny's image grow larger. When he got to the edge, she reached down to grab his fins and mask. He flashed her their father's smile, and she flashed it right back at him.

B.KERR

MICHEL
ERNESTO

Bastard Son of a Bitch

They say it's hard to be poor in Cuba. I say that's a half-truth – if everybody else is poor, then I contend it's harder to be rich in Cuba than poor. I, for one, have been victim of countless beatings and name-calling and have had more money and bicycles stolen from me than any five poor kids I know of. My mother can't trust anyone because they all turn out to be after her money or valuables. She stopped even trying years ago. I remember as a kid hearing her talking on the phone to her aunt before she died, and Aunt Josephine had told her she wouldn't come back to Cuba again, because it made her too sad. I think it was for the same reason.

It wasn't because my mother wasn't generous, either. She could never see a person who was hungry without fixing a care package of rice and beans and fruit, and I can't remember how many times she sent me to the pharmacy to buy medicine someone couldn't afford – even to the international clinic, where the prices were in dollars. I just recall her circle of friends getting smaller and smaller all the time. People who thought she should give them some big chunk of money for whatever project they were working on always left our house angry, and usually did their best to poison her name with everybody they knew. She had lost so much of her fortune early, doing just that – lending money to friends and family – finally, one day she got tired of being the bad one, asking for her money back.

Asking for money back – what a simple concept – 'It's my money, please repay it as you promised when I lent it to you.' Shakespeare was so right in Hamlet, when Polonius, or whoever the character was, gave the advice of 'neither a borrower nor a lender be'. We would walk to the main streets of Trinidad and invariably we would see heads turn to the side, pretending they hadn't seen us, or others turn around a hundred and eighty degrees and duck around the next corner. It was always the same; they'd borrowed money for a sure-fire business that couldn't fail. They always failed, mostly because it was much easier to borrow money than it was to get up every morning and work hard to pay it back. My mother had a thriving bed and breakfast, not because she put a sign on her door and paid the registration fees. She got up every morning and cleaned the house from top to bottom, handed out cards to every commission person she met – the ones who got five dollars a night just for bringing the guests to her – and gave each guest a gift when they left, with a card so they could pass her information on to others. She gave a tourist a free week in her house for making her a website and linking it to all of the correct travel and hospitality pages. She was usually booked a month ahead. Money makes money, everybody says. I say working hard and smart makes money, but what do I know – the bastard son of a rich bitch? It wasn't just mean kids I heard using that word about me. I heard it from all of the people I wouldn't have expected it from – usually people who owed my mother money. When they were borrowing from her, I usually got a lot of compliments – 'Michel Ernesto, I can't believe how much you've grown; your son is so handsome, Claudia – he's got your eyes, doesn't he?' Funny thing about it, my eyes are a different color than hers. When those same people couldn't, or wouldn't, pay back what they owed her, I suddenly became the brat bastard, and their kids should avoid playing with me.

I didn't much care who wanted to play with me and who didn't, anyway. I played with my mother. Sometimes we would walk over to my half-sister Edith's house, and Mom and her mother, Theresa (I liked to call her Mother Theresa, but Edith didn't like it.) would drink coffee and talk about stuff. Edith was only about two years older than me, so we had fun. She didn't have many toys – just two dolls, so I had to bring something of my own with me, but my mother wouldn't let me bring any of my good toys. Only ones that didn't have batteries or remote control. It wasn't because Mom bought me expensive things, either. It was always returning guests who brought me cool things, and Mom would always tell them they shouldn't have. She would give them free nights and meals, because she didn't like charity, and especially didn't want anybody to think she would pay them in any other way. Lots of the men would stare at her when their wives weren't looking. My mother is beautiful in every way.

When I was old enough to understand what the word bastard meant, I asked my mother about my father. She got this sort of far-away look, and said my father had left Trinidad before I was born, and she hadn't seen him since. It was Edith who showed me his picture, with our other half-sister Sandra, which they had in her house. He was the handsomest man I'd ever seen, and I saw right away that my eyes were the same color as his were. My oldest half-brother, Ergeny, looks exactly like him, so I always made a point of watching for him when we were in the market. He was always nice to me, rubbing my hair and telling me I was getting big and strong. Even after his girls were born, he still treated me the same way. I was invited to their birthday parties, and always went with Edith. My mother would send the best gifts with me. My half-sister Sandra had twin boys, too, but we didn't see them much, and she never had parties for their birthdays, at least not big ones. My mom sent clothes and shoes sometimes, but they lived on the other side of Trinidad, so we didn't bump into them as much.

My other half-brother, Fidel, didn't have children, and still lived with his mother, which some people said was strange. I don't think he's strange, at all – he's my favorite of all of my half-brothers and sisters. He's the one who taught me to swim. He always came to my birthdays, and always sat with me and listened to what was going on with me. It was Fidel who came to my house to tell me and my mom about my father dying in Colombia. He cried with her and really meant it. I tried to cry because my mother and my half-brother were crying; I had never met my father, and I had always secretly hated him. I didn't wish him dead, of course, but I didn't know why my mother cried so much that day.

I couldn't help but think Fidel liked my mother, because he held her until she had stopped crying, and then they both looked kind of uncomfortable. They weren't far apart in age, actually, but the complications were too much to even think about.

The day of the ceremony at the Batea was the day I started to think about my father in a different way. It was the first time we had actually done something as a 'family', as strange a family as it was. My father had been gone from Trinidad for nearly ten years, by then, so there had been no other reason for all of us to be in the same place at the same time.

I've been to the Batea dozens of times, since. Fidel taught me to snorkel and told me if I practiced, I could go down and visit my father's shrine, and see my little hand-print. It took me nearly three years before I could make it, but after that I could run my hand over all of the imprints, and even clean out any debris that was caught up in the coral. It really did look like it belonged there, part of the natural coral around it, and most of the time there were little fish swimming around in it like it was real.

It was sometime after I dove down and saw the little monument that I started to get interested in my father, and specifically, what really happened to him in Colombia. I'd finished junior high school, or what there was of it, anyway. If there was a teacher in the classroom three days a week it was a miracle, and I could have passed the exams without ever having gone to school at all. One of my classmates had a hundred percent average in all of her classes, since she'd started secondary school. And I wouldn't trust her to take care of a pet cockroach, she had so little common sense. The education system in Cuba had fallen so far since Russia stopped sending money and supplies that you either had to laugh or cry, depending on whether you were the students who got perfect marks without learning anything, or the teachers who lost part of their almost non-existent salary if any student got a failing grade. The important thing, as everybody knew, and nobody ever said out loud, was that the average grades in Cuba remained higher than those to the north. The same went for every statistic they could come up with – infant mortality, as another example, was only

162

recorded at the highest levels in Cuba. Doctors couldn't write that on a certificate, or their jobs were in jeopardy. "The baby fell, the baby had heart failure, the baby choked on its mother's breast milk." Basically, they could write anything they dreamed up, just so long as it wasn't infant mortality.

So I decided to take the route most common in my free education, and I entered the prep school for tourism and hospitality, since the family bed and breakfast was going to be mine one day. As it turned out, I actually really liked it – I learned to cook, learned to clean properly, even the correct way to make a bed and a Mojito, and I don't mean the watered-down ones they sell in the Escalenata and the Casa de la Trova. All of the tricks they play there to make extra money from the unsuspecting Yumas I would learn when I did my practice time at the Casa de la Musica. There was more money made there on a bottle of rum than three good New York accountants could calculate. Even as a rookie, when they divided the tips and, let's just say, 'other' earnings, I would walk out of there with twenty Chavitos in my pocket – the bartenders would regularly rake in closer to a hundred each. Then again, they were the magicians. For every drink a Yuma bought a ginetera, or horseback rider, for lack of a more vulgar definition, they would switch the rum bottle for one filled with water and split the take with the person who managed to get the Yuma to pay for it. There were some amazing actors in that bunch –

no doubt about that. A twenty five year old mulato man who knew how to dance, and most of them were professionals from one hotel show or another, could slide in beside a lady tourist more than twice his age, and without even speaking the language, convince her she was exactly the profile of woman he liked most, and could sweep her off her feet with three dances. He'd have her drooling over him by the time Fat Alba stood in for her set of three songs, and the best part was they almost always pulled out their own money when the first drinks were ordered, so the tourist wouldn't suspect she was just another pawn in the game. By the end of the night he'd either have an invitation home with her, where there'd be a wink to the bartender that he'd stop by the following day for his 'commission', or she'd have a note with his address and personal information for the invitation letter for the 'visit' to her country. The other money-maker was the soda scam – in the downtown shops, a can of cola or lemon drink cost fifty cents, but in the clubs they were a dollar for a Cuban, and up to two dollars for a Yuma who didn't know better. There was no sense in letting the state skim off all of that cream, so the bartenders would bring in their backpacks full of sodas, and keep the profit from the sale for themselves. The latest one I'd heard of was injecting tap water into the bottom of the purified water bottles, and then resealing them with a lighter.

Anything connected to tourism was the cash cow in Cuba – the reason for the saying that it was like an upside-down pyramid – the people in the real world who had the most, in Cuba had the least -- the people who had the lowliest positions in the hotels, cleaning rooms or even attending bathrooms, in Cuba had big houses with flat screen televisions and cars in the garage. My mother has two close doctor friends, married to each other, and it's very common for them to eat their only meal of the week with any meat in it in our house. Their shoes are sewn together with patches and you could read a book through their uniforms. The director of the Trinidad hospital, a gifted and caring doctor who commonly attends patients at his home after spending eighteen hours at the hospital – besides his turn of "guard duty" of twenty-four hours at the office without leaving – makes more money whittling dancers out of discarded blocks of wood he buys from the carpenters who work for the government (who make more money selling discarded blocks to the doctor than as carpenters). And so on, and so on. We call it the "lucha" the never-ending battle to scrounge enough out of a day, buying something for two pesos and selling it where there's a shortage for three or four, so there'll be meat on the table three or four times a week. More often than not, it's a "boneless chicken", the Cuban name for an egg.

A university professor I know from Santa Clara told me the story of how he spent sixteen weekends riding his bicycle out into the country every Saturday morning, helping a friend there to cultivate and harvest vegetables, in order to raise the ten American dollars he needed for a new pair of jeans to wear to teach English. When he'd finally saved up the ten dollars, he learned the jeans had gone up to twelve dollars, and when he'd made four more trips to the country to gather enough vegetables for the inflated price of the jeans, the front tire on his bicycle wore out from the trips, and was worth more than the jeans.

I know I'm lucky – I could eat meat five times a day if I wanted to – so naturally I prefer rice and beans. Most of my friends think I'm crazy, because they salivate just passing by a cow grazing on the side of the road. I'm sure it's just a natural desire to want what we can't have.

I saw how Fidel kept looking over at my mother, even at the Batea the day we presented the coral reef tribute to my father. I could tell it wasn't anything normal, and I knew he wasn't married, and didn't have a girlfriend I had heard about. It was when I noticed the way she looked back at him that I felt that sort of electric shock run through me. I wasn't even ten years old, then, but I already knew my mother's 'looks' better than even she did. I knew when she was happy or sad within a minute of seeing her face in the morning, and I'd heard her crying into her pillow on too many occasions. I could tell when she hugged me a little too close or longer than usual, and when she stroked my cheek after she gave me a kiss on my way to school, I prepared for the house to be spotless when I got home. She always cleaned when she was melancholy, and I can tell you that our house was seldom untidy.

I shouldn't have, and I knew it was wrong, but years later, when I noticed Fidel walking around our part of the city, I followed my mother when she left the house for 'un mandado' – the Cuban way of saying, I'm going out somewhere for something that's none of your concern. I was only fourteen at the time, but in Cuba we grow up fast on the streets, and when our hormones call, we have very little to keep us from answering. I knew it wasn't natural that my beautiful young mother was always alone, when she could have had any man she showed her teeth to. When I saw her head in the direction I'd seen my half-brother going not fifteen minutes earlier, I felt my heart-rate jump, and almost decided not to follow. But another part of me had to do it. I'd played enough games of hide and seek on these streets that I knew every entry that could possibly shelter me if she turned to look, which she didn't. She walked quickly and with purpose, barely acknowledging the people she passed along the way.

She turned onto a narrow street where the cobblestones were washed out of their normal pattern by the currents from the rain of the week before. It had a steep grade, heading up toward "La Cueva" hotel and where some people took a shortcut to get to the nightclub that was built into a natural cave. I remembered then that my mother had lived on this same street before her aunt died and left the big house to her. Could it be possible we still owned the old place? I got my answer sooner than I expected, when I rounded the corner just in time to see the door open a crack, and I recognized Fidel's shirt and shorts from earlier, even though he didn't show his face. My mother slipped inside, and they closed the door.

I don't know how long I stood there, staring at the closed door, before I returned to our house. The first things I saw when I walked in the door were the fading pictures of the five siblings and my father's five exes. I can't explain it, but that was when I cried for the first time – I hadn't shed a single tear for my father when we learned of his death in Colombia, or even at the Batea, when everyone else, even half of the fishermen, had constantly wiped their eyes. I looked again and again at the picture of the five of us, and there was something about it that bothered me. I remember just as they were about to take the picture that my mother told me to smile, and I'd looked over at her just as the picture was snapped from another angle. Sandra, Ergeny and Edith looked at the camera with their somber faces. Fidel's eyes were focused on something else – the same thing as mine... even back then, Fidel was infatuated with my mother. Maybe even already in love with her. I kept looking at his eyes, knowing they were looking at my mother, and I felt like I could see right into his soul.

I was spread out on my bed, pretending to be watching who-knows-what on the television when I heard the front door open and the little bell tinkle. My mother came straight to where I was to show me the avocados she had bought for dinner. I pretended they were the best ones I'd ever seen. I guess I was a little over-enthusiastic, because she asked me if something was wrong. I squeezed her hand and told her I was just tired. There was something about catching my mother in a lie that made me wonder how many more she had told me before this one, and how many of the truths of my entire life I could be sure of.

But, with my own brother?

Sometime during those two hours that I feigned sleeping while I listened to her hum in the kitchen as she prepared the evening meal of rice, beans, and the world's best avocados, I had a fundamental shift in my heart. The pendulum of my sentiments slipped from one hundred percent mother and zero percent father to maybe ninety-five percent and five percent. Nothing dramatic – I wasn't going to stop loving my mother because she had hidden a part of her life from me for obvious reasons. What was significant about it was for the very first time in my life, I wondered what my father might have thought about something – anything. My father had sprouted a tiny root in the garden that was my conscience.

I recalled how at the Batea that day, years earlier, when the rest of the family cried and talked about my father, I hadn't shed a tear, or even felt the slightest twinge of sorrow that he was dead. He meant less than nothing to me. He'd gone from my mother's life long before I was even born, and of all of the five siblings' hand-prints in the monument, mine were the only ones that didn't share his last name. I only stuck my hand in that concrete because it had looked like fun.

It was like my heart felt like it needed to share the betrayal with someone else – someone who might feel even more hurt than I did. I thought about my other half-sisters and -brothers. I even considered telling Sandra, to see what she would think, but I knew it would just be more negativity for my mother. Somehow it would be her fault. I decided the person most likely to share my sentiments was the object of nearly fifteen years of my own hatred – my father. My father. MY father!

When I couldn't pretend to be interested in the only program on television – farm workers smiling while they labored in the hot sun, proud of the fact they had once again harvested a record crop of black beans – I started my own list of lies. I told my mother I was going to see a buddy for a while before dinner, and grabbed my mountain bike from the rack behind the front door. I left in the direction of my friend's house, but instead made a few extra turns and ended up in the Barranca, at Theresa' and Edith's house. I knew of all the rest, these were the two people in the world who most loved my father, and for some reason I had a need to understand why.

It was Edith who gave me the most insight into who the man was – she couldn't stop talking about him, as though he was her hero. The truth was, she had no real memory of him, either. She was an infant the day he left the house to dive and never returned. Everything she told me about her father and his grand exploits came from second-hand tidbits she'd picked up from our other siblings and, of course, from her constant questions to her mother, Theresa. Whereas my mother had closed the book on my father when he left, Theresa, on the other hand, made the choice to build him up as someone special to her child. In my house there were no pictures of my father, but here there were only two – one with Sandra and the barracuda, and another smaller one of Ergeny with Edith in his arms, the day they'd arrived from the hospital. He had his amazing smile in both pictures. Fathers and daughters – there was always something special between them. Edith talked on and on about how he'd been such an amazing diver, the stories about the barracuda and others she'd committed to memory.

By the time I'd left their house, several hours later, I felt like I had just met him for the first time. Theresa had loved him more than I'd ever imagined, and seemed to pity him more than resent him for his defects. After all, he'd gotten her friend pregnant with me while he was still married to her. If anyone had reason to be bitter about Ergeny, surely it was Theresa. There was nothing of the sort, though. Her face lit up when she recounted stories of their short time together, and she spoke of the rest of us as though we were all a part of her own family. Even though she was black and from an entirely different background from the rest of us, she called Sandra, who was a few years younger than she was, her oldest step-daughter. The same went for my half-brothers Ergeny and Fidel. To Theresa, we were all part of her family – even me. Never once had she ever looked at me sideways, as the child of her husband's mistress, and a mistress who was supposedly her friend. To her, these were just commas and periods in the story that was her life. Instead of feeling like I'd learned what I needed, though, I felt hungry for more. I went home making plans for the next lie I would tell my mother, of where I'd be when in reality I would be finding my way to Ergeny Junior's ranch near the Batea. For some reason, the name Junior had stayed with him, even though there was no longer a Senior. A lot of the people who had known our father well had shortened it to just Junior.

That night I'd packed my swimming gear and froze three plastic bottles of water. I set the cooler beside the front door, as I always had when I planned to spend a day at the beach. I even went so far as to fake an entire phone conversation with my buddy Felix so my mother would hear me planning the day at the beach. She insisted on making her famous pasta to spread on the sandwiches for both of us and found my biggest beach towel, so we could share it. It was a combination of boiled pork or chicken, which ever she had available, spaghetti, onion, garlic, red peppers and tomato sauce. She knew it was my favorite. I couldn't help thinking she was probably preparing a nice picnic herself for the next day, since I'd be out of her hair for the day. No doubt she was making sandwiches for four back there in the kitchen, singing along to Polo Montanez' 'Guajiro Natural', one of her favorites.

I couldn't help thinking how we were becoming very good at this deception game.

The following morning I was up early, loading the cooler with water and the sandwiches and dressed in my beach clothes. I told my mother I was meeting Felix at his place, where we'd hire the' maquina' – the Cuban name for the pre-sixties cars that we rented to take us to the beach or anywhere else we needed to go. She seemed to have been up for a while by then, and had braided her hair already. Obviously, she had plans of her own. I grabbed the cooler and towel and headed toward Felix's house, after giving her a kiss and hug and telling her I'd be careful. I passed his place and continued another two blocks to the street that led to the bus terminal, where the private taxis congregated. I found a car to take me to the Batea for 8 dollars, and would wait for as long as I needed for another four, and then home for an additional 8. I told him I didn't mind if he left me there and came back a few hours later, so he could make a few extra trips in the middle, but I wanted the car to myself both ways. He asked me to show him the twenty bucks first, probably not convinced a kid like me actually had the money. I had the other eighty dollars hidden in a flap in my wallet – I didn't like showing too much money when I paid for something, but I always had extra cash in case I needed it. Ergeny had told me on the phone when I'd called that he'd be home all day, and I should plan on eating lunch with him and the family. His girls were getting bigger, and Ergeny's wife was really cool, so I'd agreed. When we pulled into his steep driveway, half an hour later, his friendly wave assured me he was happy to see me. He whistled sharply and his two big guard dogs rushed to his side, where he grabbed their collars, just to be sure. He lived in an isolated area, so the dogs were a necessary evil to protect his family and property. At nearly thirty, Ergeny looked like a twenty-year-old, his arms and chest and stomach all solid muscle. His skin was as dark as Edith's, although he had no mixture of races to thank for it. It was eighteen hours a day in the Cuban sun that had bronzed him permanently. As the maquina backed around to leave, Ergeny embraced me like we hadn't seen each other in ten years, and gave me a fatherly kiss on the cheek, which made me feel more special than I wanted to admit. At nearly fifteen years my senior, he could almost have been my father, as Sandra could have been my mother, being four years older than he was. Doing all of the mathematical possibilities in my extended family would take a pretty good calculator and a degree in computer science.

After kissing the cheeks of his wife and the two girls, and their cousin on his wife's side, who had been staying with them after a sudden divorce, Ergeny invited me to join him in his shallow pool. He'd built it the previous summer for his girls to cool off in, and had added a thatch roof to keep the sun at bay. There was even a concrete table in the middle, and a few raised blocks where we could sit with our feet in the cool water. He offered me a beer, but I knew I'd be drunk by the time I finished the first one, so I accepted a cola drink instead. His wife headed off to fix lunch in the outdoor kitchen twenty meters from the pool, and the girls returned to the program they'd been watching when I'd arrived.

Ergeny tried to set me at ease, making small talk about fishing and the weather, but I stopped him as quickly as I could. I explained I hadn't come to see him as a casual visit, even though I knew I should do that more often. I'd come because I wanted to know more about who our father was, and whatever details he could or would share about the strange circumstances surrounding his death. I even apologized for my lack of interest in the past about the subject, and he nodded his understanding of my unique situation in the family. I saw the Hollywood smile change ever-so-slightly as he started to formulate answers in his head – answers that meant dredging up things he'd long-since put to rest. When he

started, though, he seemed to be talking to a
therapist, instead of a bastard half-brother. He
started out sharing the few memories he had of his
father at home. There couldn't have been many,
since he had been three years old when Ergeny
Senior had left him and his mother for Fidel's
mother, whom he'd met at a diving competition.
He told me how he remembered his father tossing
him in the air and catching him with his strong
arms and hands. He remembered the smell of fish
and the ocean when his father held him to his
chest.

I don't know why I felt my eyes swelling with
tears when he mentioned the memory of his
father's smell. For sure it wasn't because I would
have liked the odor of fish and salt water. I think
it was just something about having a memory of
him at all that hit me. I had no memories of my
own father, whereas Edith and Ergeny had
something, anything. In my mind, I could feel his
strong arms holding me and I could see his
laughing eyes and bright white smile as he caught
me before I fell.

Ergeny noticed I had lapsed into an inward
moment, and slapped me on the knee, changing
the subject. He asked me if I'd mind sharing my
sandwiches with his girls while we waited for our
lunch. They didn't get to eat much that they
didn't raise on his little ranch, as he called it, so
the pasta spread would be a big treat for them. I
was glad to see my mother had included two
orange soft drinks with the water, and I saw the

bright smiles on the girls' faces as they dug into the sandwiches. Had she known I was coming here, my mother would surely have sent clothes or shoes for the girls, too. Ergeny knew I had come without her knowledge right away. He was as wise as he was handsome. I was amazed at how he could look like he belonged on a magazine cover when he had been feeding his pigs and chickens minutes before I'd arrived.

When I got the nerve to ask him to tell me more about our father's death in Colombia, he gave me the surprise I wasn't expecting. He looked at me with his piercingly dark eyes, and the permanent grin on his face disappeared, just for an instant. He stared at a little bug that struggled in the water between the two of us for about fifteen seconds before he responded.

"I don't believe he's dead." With that bomb dropped, he stepped out of the water and walked barefoot to the old refrigerator, and pulled out a cold beer. From a home-built shelf above it, he pulled out a file of papers, and called me to join him at the table there.

I'd taken his place, watching the bug struggling to right itself, and couldn't help but feel like that had been me, after hearing what Ergeny had just told me. For some reason, I scooped it up and set it on the concrete table before I shook my feet and slipped into my store-bought leather sandals to join him at the table. I had never liked the taste of beer when my older friends had offered them to me at parties or at the beach. I was too young to drink, anyway, still, but here with Ergeny, who looked like he had just climbed out of the picture in Edith's living room, something told me that having a beer with my big brother was the right thing to do, and I reached for his and took a long swallow. It was bitter and made my eyes water, but I was having it with this man who was a legend to most people in Trinidad ever since the gold watch thing when he was about my age. It reminded me I had done nothing to gain the respect of, well, anyone, so far in my life, and Ergeny had a ranch overlooking the ocean, with a wife and two beautiful daughters. I needed to spend more time with him, and less watching television, I decided.

He'd replaced his beer, and wiped his hands on an old towel that hung on a wire stretched between two poles that supported the thatched roof over the outdoor kitchen and dining area. Then he moved over to sit beside me on the bench and opened the folder to the first of dozens of loose pages. I was shocked to see it was a page torn from a newspaper, but not the Granma we all received in Cuba. This was a fancy paper from somewhere in Colombia. The headline that Ergeny had circled read 'Kidnapping Ring Busted'. I looked from the headline to Ergeny's face. With a slight twist of his head and a shift in his gaze, he signaled me to read more of the story. It didn't take long before I recognized the details of the group that had concentrated their efforts on the Cubans who tried to escape through Ecuador at the time there had been free passage to that country. There was even mention of the bridge where they had assassinated a number of their victims. One of them, on condition of anonymity, had given up the others to the police. That person had been Cuban. I read the story twice, while Ergeny watched my eyes move back and forth, studying my reaction to the most important passages. I could tell he had memorized the words himself. When I looked up at him again, he slipped the article to the back of the stack, and the next paper jumped off the page at me. It was another newspaper article, this time from Bolivia, and at first I didn't make any connection. The story was about a local festival, and there were a series of pictures of people dancing in elaborate costumes with feathers. Ergeny saw my confusion, and pulled the first newspaper article from the back of the pile again, and just pointed to the date – July 15th, 1991 – a few months before I was born. Then he placed the second paper in front of me and had me point out the date. It was roughly six months later. So what? Ergeny was playing a game with me I didn't much enjoy. He pointed to the bottom of the page, where it advised the story continued in another section. We flipped through to that page, where several more photos filled the entire two page spread. Festival queen, prize animals of every sort, fishing derby winners, and assorted children with smiling, toothless faces. Nothing grabbed my attention. What did it mean?

Ergeny had obviously spent a lot of time studying this file. It was discolored from dirty fingers and constant movements of the pages. He flicked his eyes again toward the fish derby picture, and this time I saw what he had seen. The winner, with his string of fish hanging from his raised arm to the ground, had the same face as the person beside me at the table. I immediately searched the caption for the name Ergeny, but didn't find it anywhere. Then Ergeny grabbed my hand, with my index finger under his own, and passed it under the name of the winner. Michel Ernesto Gonzalez. It still didn't register in my brain. He passed my finger under the name Michel Ernesto again, and then twisted my hand until it pointed at my own chest. Michel Ernesto. A warmth passed through me like a ghost had just danced on my chest, and a lump formed in my throat. I thought of saying something, anything, but knew I had forgotten how to speak. I reached for the beer and finished it. How? I was an infant at the time this picture was taken. He shouldn't have ever known what my name was, because my mother named me after her aunt's father, in her honor. My name had nothing to do with Ergeny or anyone connected to him.

Without any further urging from Ergeny, I flipped through the stack of pages. Some of them I could figure out the meaning without help, and others I just had to look at him and he would point out the significant passages or pictures. It was like Dora Exploradora from the morning cartoons. He even had a map of South America pasted into the front cover of the folder, with circles around cities he'd found evidence our father had been in. I sat shoulder-to-shoulder with Ergeny, following the trail around South America the dead man had taken. As would have been expected, he had settled in coastal cities, where he could earn his living from the ocean.

And earn his living was exactly what Ergeny Senior had done, as the other documents proved. Somehow Junior had gotten his hands on statements from the bank in Trinidad, where regular deposits had been made into two accounts. One was in the name of Edith, and the other in the name of Michel Ernesto.

I could feel my hands trembling as I stared at the columns of numbers. With only two children left under twenty-one, the deposits had been substantial, and the totals at the bottom were astonishing. My mind kept returning to the name Michel Ernesto. It meant that not only had my father been alive, but he had first-hand knowledge of Trinidad since I'd been born, and with the bank deposits still in my hands, I had the proof of something that an hour earlier was only a childish fantasy. Not only that, but he had taken MY name. First sons were normally given the honor of sharing their father's first name. I was sitting beside the living proof of that.

I watched Ergeny's wife peel the dirty, thick skin from a small pile of malanga – potato-like roots that gave substance and vitamins to beans or soup. Many a child in Cuba had grown up healthy and strong thanks to a steady diet of malanga. I could see the garden through a space in the trees, and knew there was malanga growing there. The remnants would be fed to the half dozen pigs they raised for their own use and to sell when they needed cash for other staples or clothes for the girls.

"Why didn't you tell us earlier?" was the only thing I could manage after I'd closed the file as gently as I could, with the pages back into their original order.

"I wanted to be sure, really sure, before I let everybody know."

"But this is more than sure, with the bank deposits alone," I countered.

"I know. That was a lie, really." He paused, finished his beer, and went for another, offering me one, but I wanted my wits about me, and declined. "I've been trying to contact him, actually... before."

I imagined how difficult it would have been for Ergeny to use limited resources to make international calls on cell phones to operators who would have put him on terminal hold while they looked for numbers registered to a Michel Ernesto Gonzalez. Dollars ticking away by the minute until they either came back on the line to tell him there was nothing registered, or his credit expired waiting. Every phone call represented a month of food for his girls.

"Do any of the others know?"

"I've discussed it with Sandra, and I think she met with Fidel. I haven't mentioned anything to Theresa and Edith. You know how Theresa feels about our father. This would probably send her over the bend."

I thought about how all of us knew Theresa had never stopped loving Ergeny, no matter what had happened – no matter that he had slept with one of her friends, my mother. No matter that he had left without a word or a kiss or a hug or even a note to explain why. I wondered what news like this might do to her – if it would be positive or negative – and Edith... he was her fallen hero – her personal Che.

Saved by the call to eat, we could take our minds off of our father while we ate fish Ergeny had speared early in the morning before I'd arrived, lightly breaded and seared with thin slices of garlic; a soup like none I'd eaten before, thick with malanga and carrots and peppers, all harvested from their own garden hours earlier. I noticed Ergeny's wife had paused to pray silently before serving the meal, and it gave me some hope that Cuba could come back from its Godless state with time. Looking around at the bounty my half-brother had amassed – animals and gardens full of vegetables, trees full of fruit of every variety imaginable, and two beautiful daughters, and I compared it to our own luxury. Both of us were rich, but in very different ways. I could see the pride in Ergeny's eyes as he watched me devour the fish and soup and rice and beans, and the guava marmalade with home-made cheese. 'From thy bounty, through Christ, our Lord, Amen' popped into my mind at that moment, and I felt a pride in my family like never before.

Finishing the dessert, watching the girls with their perfect manners and the pretty, matching dresses they'd changed into for the meal, I suddenly felt very sorry for our father, who art in South America somewhere, because he couldn't sit at this rustic table with this beautiful family and with the two sons who shared his first name. I listened to the sounds that came out of the forest around us, mixed with the animals that grazed and grunted and squawked and buzzed. There were odors, good and bad, that ebbed and flowed with the ocean breeze that wafted through the trees. I lived in an immaculate home, full of ornamental beauty and luxury, but we didn't have what Ergeny had – not even close.

When I'd finished the dessert, and the girls had cleared the dishes from the table, I asked Ergeny why he had done all of this – the investigation – the expensive phone calls, paying for internet time in the tourist cafes in Trinidad. He answered by just glancing toward his daughters.

"Family," was all he said. My eyes once again puffed with tears, and I felt my lips trembling, even though I had them pinned tightly between my teeth.

My visit with Ergeny had come to an end. A lot of things in my life had come to an end, I couldn't help but think, as I gathered the girls into my arms for a long hug and a promise to come back to visit soon. I don't know where the idea came from, not having ever set foot inside the five-hundred-year-old Catholic church, overlooking the main park in the Historic Center of the city; but when Ergeny's wife came to me with her outstretched arms, I asked her if she would give me her blessing, which made her stop and search my eyes to see if I was making a joke at her expense. She must not have seen anything, though, because she touched my forehead with a gentleness that made me shiver, while she moved her lips in a silent blessing and a short prayer.

The diesel engine of the maquina brought me back to the present, and Ergeny and I walked together to where it choked and sputtered and spit little rocks as the driver maneuvered the metal dinosaur to face back where it had come from.

In contrast to my visit with Edith and Theresa, where I'd encountered exactly what I'd been expecting – unwavering devotion and reverence, here with Ergeny I would leave with the last thing I had been looking for – hope. Sandra had once told me how sorry she felt for Ergeny Junior, being so much like his father in every way, and yet having had probably the worst relationship. Next to mine, of course, but sometimes no relationship is worlds better than a bad one.

I extended my hand to my handsome half-brother, and he batted it away and pulled me to his barrel chest, kissing me on the cheek the way a father would, like when I'd arrived. I felt his powerful arms and thought about how safe they must make his wife and daughters feel.

For some reason, I asked the driver to turn left instead of right out of Ergeny's driveway, to take me to the Batea, just for a few minutes. I remembered the cold water and the thermos of coffee my mother had packed, and something told me to pour some of each into the ocean water, an offering to my father, fifty yards from the underwater altar. Even if he wasn't dead, and wasn't anywhere near Cuba, the oceans were all connected, and I felt like he was more likely underwater than out of it, wherever he was.

I looked out over the ocean for a long while, noticing the few boats that hadn't yet returned from their night of fishing, remembering the sight of dozens of them anchored here so many years earlier. That made me think about the pictures we took that day, and that made me think about Fidel looking at my mother, and that made me think about the lies I'd already told her, and those yet to tell.

Marco Antonio Solis crooned over the radio as I opened the door to our house forty minutes later. That was a good sign. I could see the house had been cleaned and dusted. That was a bad sign. It was becoming difficult to read my mother, now that we had tangled ourselves in the web of mutual deception. It was as I slipped into my house sandals that I heard another voice besides my mother's coming from the kitchen. I strained my ears, trying to match the voice, which was very familiar, to a face. My mental computer ran through the people who visited most, but none of them registered. The computer was malfunctioning, because the voice didn't belong to this house at all. It was my half-sister, Sandra, sitting in my chair at my table, drinking coffee with my mother. I felt like Baby Bear, returning to find Goldilocks sleeping in her bed. I guess the eyeballs bouncing from one to the other like a tennis rally in fast-forward, must have looked comical to them, because they shared a laugh between them. It was probably a necessary one, because I could see both of them had been crying not long before.

Naturally, the first thing my mother asked me was how I had enjoyed the beach. I should have remembered to have at least taken my shirt off so that it looked like I'd gotten a bit of sun, but I just told her I'd had a good day, which wasn't a lie, sort of. She explained that Sandra had called soon after I'd gone to come by and see her, and they'd been talking ever since. I could only speculate as to the subject of their five hours of conversation since I'd been gone.

"You saved me a trip," I began. "I was hoping to visit with you tomorrow, if you were going to be home."

She told me she'd be home all day, and I was most welcome. I should spend the afternoon, so I could play with the twins after their naps. My curiosity was killing me. What did Sandra know about Fidel, and what had she told my mother about our father? The worst part was I couldn't tell either of them what I knew, or I'd reveal my own lies. Sandra broke the tension by hugging and kissing me, and telling me she'd see me tomorrow. She hugged my mother, too, and by the way each of them held onto each other's hands afterwards, it appeared they had shared something big and important.

I didn't need to wait long after Sandra left before my mother made a sweeping motion with her arm and hand, inviting me to join her at the table. The look in her eyes was enough to tell me she was waiting for an explanation from me. I did my best to return the same look to her, and we formed our own little Mexican standoff at our dining room table. We were saved by a knock at the door, which I jumped up to respond to, being the one who least wanted to start the conversation. It was a group of four German tourists that had arrived from Havana with their reservations in hand. Thankfully one spoke enough Spanish, and my mother enough rudimentary German to show them to their rooms and help them settle in for their week of tours and trips to the beach. I never got involved much with the guests – my mother lived for the cross-cultural banter and practicing what she'd learned from the language books she traded with different tourists. I generally kept my part of the bargain as the gopher – go fer chicken, go fer eggs, go fer water. I had to admit, though, that when I saw the teenaged girl enter, with her blond hair and shining blue eyes, I thought about picking up the German/Spanish dictionary. She looked to be close to my age, and had a much younger brother tagging along with her. She shot me one more glance as she closed the door to the bedroom behind them.

My reprise wasn't very long, though, because my mother had prepared everything ahead of time for the guests, and was back at the table within minutes, two glasses of ice-cold water in her hands, ready to pick up where we'd left off. "Which one of us should start?" She took a long drink of her water, never taking her eyes off of mine.

"I spent the day with Ergeny," I began, "learning things about my father." She indicated with her pursed lips and slight squint in her eyes that my deceit had hurt her. I opened my eyes as wide as they would go and looked as deep into hers as I could, letting her know I had every bit as much reason to be angry with her as she with me. "And I found out things I can still hardly believe."

189

"I've been getting the same education from Sandra," she responded.

"Didn't Fidel tell you?" I opened the door to let the elephant into the room. "Or did you have other things to discuss?"

She had the water glass halfway to her mouth, but set it back down and wiped her forehead with her free hand. "I suppose it's time for me to come clean, too."

"If it's not too much trouble." Probably a little too sarcastic for a fourteen-year-old. I caught the reprimand in her reaction.

"You know I've been alone since your father left – well, I've always been alone, actually." She corrected her own error, pretending as she had that my father was ever really with her. "I can't really say when it happened, or how, but things have developed between me and Fidel."

"My half-brother, Fidel," I corrected. I wasn't going to let her off the hook on this one.

"We've been trying to keep it quiet until we knew if it was real, or just an infatuation." Now she pressed her fingers into her eye sockets, ending up with her hands covering her face and eyes completely. "I didn't want to hide anything from you, Michel Ernesto..."

I wondered if she was waiting for me to express my opinion about it, because she didn't look up from her guarded position. I even started to form my battery of reasons why it was such a bad idea, when she removed her hands, looking like she'd seen something horrible in her palms.

"I'm pregnant, Honey."

I wondered if it was me, or if the house was actually crumbling around me, folding in on itself, colors changing before my eyes. I don't know what the look on my face told her, but it brought her to tears, sobbing almost silently, probably from years of practice. My reaction was my usual – I got up from the table and headed for my room, almost bumping into the German family who had already changed their clothes to head out to explore the city. The daughter looked fantastic in shorts and a tight tee-shirt and white tennis shoes. I was in no mood to take much notice, though, and probably seemed rude, not saying a word as they passed. My room was up the stairs, next to my mother's, but when she had guests my mother slept in the spare room next to the kitchen to be more attentive to their needs, and also to keep an eye on the expensive antiques that were tempting to anyone who happened by when the doors were open.

Those three words echoed through the entire house as I closed and locked my door behind me, something I did on very few occasions. When my mother asked me through the door if I was coming down for dinner two hours later, I told her I was still full from the lunch I'd had with Ergeny and his family. She knew how I was when I was upset, and didn't insist. It wouldn't have done any good.

The next morning, I showered early and left the house without a word to anyone. I'd seen some new toys in the Universo shop across the street from the Copelia where they used to sell ice cream, but now it was just one more place to pay too much for beer, because it was necessary to have a place for the tourists to spend money every thirty steps in the city. It was before eight, and the shops didn't open their doors until nine, so I found a pizza seller and grabbed the folded bread by the pieces of brown paper, and slipped next door into the Rapidito to buy a cold orange juice. Albertico had worked there for years, now, and even though he was as big as a house, he'd never lost the "tico" suffix from his name, indicating he was the son of another Alberto. He always had a smile and a bone-breaking handshake for me when I came by. I liked to sit in the park on the wooden benches, watching the "lucha" – the battle, as we Cubans called it. The everyday struggle to keep heads above water, and try to put away something for a rainy day. There were a lot of rainy days, unfortunately. I was exempt from the lucha, myself, never having had to wonder where my next meal would come from. Sometimes I envied my fellow Cubans, who all shared a common foe – hunger and boredom. Nobody moved very fast in their battle, and there always seemed to be time to stop and share their latest problems with friends or neighbors they came in contact with. My mother and I, on the other hand, were more like spectators in the never-ending show that was survival in Cuba. One of the people who dedicated himself to renting movies and foreign television programs had a series called 'Survivor', where the protagonists were left to their own devices to win a large amount of money if they were the last to drop out of the program. Immediately the comparisons began, where the Cuban people laughed and suggested they try dropping these soft Americans into Cuba with a doctor's monthly salary here and see how long any of them would make it.

I didn't know much about cars, but I liked to see how well the old relics had been restored and maintained. With the fanciest hotel in town, the Iberostar, in front of the park, there was always a good selection of the classic Chevrolets and Fords to admire. That was another thing I never had any desire to own. I had a great mountain bike my mother had bought from a tourist when he left for home a year earlier, but even so I put many more miles on my sneakers than on my bike. I saw a couple of kids from my school and waved back to them when they nodded their recognition. I know I shouldn't have, but I tossed a few scraps of my pizza to the two scrawny dogs that hung around, hoping for a tidbit. With extra food as scarce as it was in Cuba, lately, it wasn't a good time to be a street dog. From a distance, I spotted the German family getting onto the open tour bus that made its rounds of Trinidad, pointing out museums and other landmarks. They didn't see me, or at least didn't let on that they did. The daughter looked bored from the distance I saw them from.

When I noticed people filing into the shops, I checked my watch and saw it was nearly nine-fifteen. I'd people-watched longer than I'd thought. I tossed my juice box and the brown papers from the pizza into the overflowing garbage receptacle beside the downturned cannon that symbolized Cuba's peaceful intentions, and headed to the little hole-in-the-wall toy shop on the corner. I'd seen plastic baseball bats and gloves there a few days ago, and bought two matching sets in different colors for the twins. I thought about calling a bici-taxi to take me to Sandra's house, but decided it wasn't more than twenty blocks from the center where I was, and the sun wasn't too high in the sky yet. I'd take some of the side streets that weren't as familiar to me. I loved the colonial architecture, and it was a hobby of mine to take note of unusually traditional properties when I was walking around the city. Sadly, the economic and political situation in Cuba dictated that most of the best places had been divided by divorce or pure commerce, with doors and windows added where they didn't belong, and general disregard for the esthetic values of the original construction. Our house was one of the best examples in the city of the preservation of the original style, inside and out.

Sandra had asked me to wait until the afternoon so I could play with the boys after their naps, but I knew she would be at home now. She didn't go to the Candonga until after lunch, so we'd have time to talk before then. It was already a scorcher of a day, with humidity in the nineties, so I made sure I chose the shaded sidewalks on my way. I was thankful it was downhill from the park to Jose Mendoza School, and the breeze coming off of the ocean had made it to the streets of Trinidad, not enough to cool me completely, but it kept the damage to a minimum. Once I arrived at the corner where the school was, it was only a few more blocks to Sandra's house, but I'd pass directly in front of Fidel's place to get there. I quietly hoped I wouldn't accidently stumble upon him. I wasn't ready for any sort of a confrontation with my half-brother-step-father. I shuddered when I tried to figure out how many hyphens their child was going to have – half-brother-half-nephew? I'd need to sit down with a pen and paper for that one.

Luckily, I saw the door and window tightly closed when I passed by Fidel's house. I shouldn't have speculated where he was, but I couldn't help it.

At Sandra's place, I could hear the music coming from her stereo long before I got to the door. She was the local DJ for the entire community, and was always happy to keep things lively. When I got to the door I saw her dancing in the kitchen with her t-shaped cleaning stick and cloth – in Cuba they call it an aragan, which is roughly translated to lazy guy. If Cubans were anything, it was clean. Almost daily the floors were cleaned wall-to-wall, and on Saturdays it was common to see the sidewalks in front of every home gleaming with water, because it was the only day people were allowed to throw water outside into the streets. Any other day of the week, and they could be fined for using excess water. I could hear the familiar hissing of the pressure cooker when there was a lull in the music – probably beans for lunch today – and two kittens chased the cleaning mop back and forth as she made her floors shine.

When she looked up and saw me standing in the doorway, she was a little surprised, but didn't look upset in any way. In her mid-thirties, Sandra was still a very attractive woman, and had kept in shape chasing her twins around. She'd cut her long hair to above her shoulders, probably to avoid the extra time it took to care for it now that she had the boys. Ergeny Junior was like a walking clone of our father, and Edith was like a brown female version, but the rest of us only had pieces of him, like a puzzle that had been divided into three and shared equally among us. Sandra was taller than I was, and had his athletic body and tiny ears, while Fidel favored his mother, but had Ergeny's eyes and the dimple on his right cheek. People said I had the same walk as he did, even though I'd never seen him walk – or sit, or stand. I'd only known him to run, ironically.

I set the bag of toys on the wicker rocking chair next to the teaming bookshelf. I could see one place that Sandra had spent some of her windfall. By the look of the titles and thickness of some of the hardcover books, she was into classics. The television above the bookshelf was modern and had a DVD player attached to it. I could imagine her watching old movies while she crocheted at night. There was a hum of an air conditioner coming from where the twins still slept, probably in the same room as her mother.

Sandra wrapped me in her long arms and I could feel her kissing the top of my head, as she would have done with her own boys. It felt better than I remembered from the last time I'd visited. Family was a good thing, I reminded myself -- no matter how tangled the branches of the tree might be. I noticed a brilliant green gecko clinging to the bars of the window that led to the walkway beside the house. It seemed to be looking back at me as it puffed its neck into a big bubble. 'Lookin' for love in all the wrong places' popped into my head – a song in English that I'd learned in school. The teacher used songs and poetry to help us remember better. I laughed to myself, remembering how Pedro Arturo, the class clown, had belted it out in front of the group, while lifting Tamara's skirt with a ruler.

Cuba teamed with little remnants of the dinosaur age, starting with the world's most aggressive crocodiles that could jump ten feet in the air for a chunk of meat, to the most amazing chameleons that would change colors to match the branch or wall they perched on. There were inside creatures – the salamander-like animals that were almost transparent – they would sometimes live in a single room in a house for years. I had one in my bedroom I called Art, because it hid behind the big mural that hung on the wall opposite my bed. I could never remember Art not being there, and I would be sad the day I didn't see him hanging around. The geckos seldom entered a house, happy to cling to the iron railings and branches of fruit trees. Then there were the little curly-tailed critters that preferred the safety of little caves in rocks or water drains. They could scamper up a cement wall with the best of their cousins, but seemed to prefer solid ground over branches. There were different varieties of iguana as well, but they were mostly found further east, nearer to Santiago de Cuba.

Apparently, I wasn't the gecko's type, and it scurried up the bar and leapt onto the brick fence, off to find a nice juicy bug for breakfast. A rooster with a bad sense of time crowed from behind the neighbor's fence, and when I looked back, the gecko was gone. My focus turned to the mamey tree, whose branches overhung Sandra's patio – the fruit that was on her side of the fence belonged to Sandra, and I imagined the boys enjoying a nice shake, one of my favorites. I must have read Sandra's mind, as she pulled me by the hand to the kitchen table and pulled out a pitcher of the brownish-orange drink. It tasted like heaven to me. She'd mixed the 'meat' of two mameys with powdered milk, water, sugar and ice, so it was almost frozen. I felt slightly embarrassed by my eagerness, drinking the glass she'd poured in one long, satisfying gulp. She immediately filled the glass a second time, and I was determined to make this one last at least as long as the one she'd poured herself.

"I don't want to drink the boys' breakfast," I said, holding my hand over my glass.

"This pitcher I made just for you and me," she responded, opening the fridge to reveal another entire pitcher. "I make theirs with less sugar, to keep them from flying away."

I excused myself to wash my hands – in Cuba only family even think about using the bathroom in a house that isn't their own. I hadn't used the bathroom in Sandra's house since I could remember, so the surprise that awaited me when I entered was no small thing. When I turned on the lights, I was surrounded by images of our father – Sandra had paid someone to paint the three pictures – her with her father and the barracuda, the five siblings and the five mothers – all transferred onto ceramic tiles triple the size of the originals. Whomever had done the work was a true artist – every detail was captured, even Fidel and me looking in the same direction. I felt like if I touched the teeth of the barracuda, I'd cut my fingers. Sandra hadn't changed her house for a bigger or better one – she'd just made her own more comfortable for her mother and twins, and spent some of it to make a personal shrine to her father and family.

She had a big smile on her face when I returned to the kitchen, and I indicated that I loved the idea. I asked her if what we now knew about our father changed anything for her. She sat there, looking up and to the left, as though her answer was written on the kitchen ceiling.

"I'd like another picture of him with his grandchildren, for the opposite wall," she said, satisfied that she had answered me honestly. I saw from her eyes she wasn't making a joke.

I served myself another glass of the mamey shake, and offered to fill hers, but she declined. A breeze blew in from the east, and brought with it the pungent odor of the pig in the next yard. It must have been the day they cleaned its pen, because it was overpowering.

"I understand you got an education from Ergeny, yesterday," Sandra began. "I know it should have been me who gave you the news. We've been discussing how to tell you and Edith."

"Fidel knows everything, too?" I must have either said it in a negative tone of voice, or had the wrong facial expression, because Sandra gave me a stern look in response to my question.

"Fidel is learning the details as we get them. We only met with him a couple of weeks ago."

"Since he's spending so much time with my mother, I assumed he would have told her." I drank half of the shake, trying to hide my negativity behind the glass.

"Michel Ernesto, it sounds to me that you have a problem with Fidel seeing your mother." Being so near in age to my mother, I always felt like Sandra was more of an aunt than a sister.

"Don't YOU have a problem with it?" I countered, no longer hiding my feelings. "He's my brother! And she's his father's ex-girlfriend."

"Would it make you feel any different if I told you that Fidel saw Claudia first?"

I looked back at her, trying to assimilate what she was saying. "What? When?"

"It was the same day, actually. Edith's first birthday celebration – remember that your mother and Theresa are school friends." I nodded my consensus. "Fidel brought the paper plates and cups for the party, while your father was off buying the cake and refreshments and arranging for Corbatica the clown. Claudia had agreed to help decorate the house for the party, so she was there when Fidel arrived with the plates. I thought he was going to walk into the kitchen wall the way he stared at your mother, who was hanging balloons from the living room light fixture. He had just turned fourteen, and she was seventeen, going on eighteen, and you know how attractive Claudia is."

"And my father?"

Sandra's expression wasn't particularly appreciative of our father. "He arrived shortly afterwards, and as always, became the center of the universe with his big smile and charisma. Even though he was already in his mid-forties, he was still a striking figure of a man, with his dark tanned skin and full head of black hair. I remember he wore a white silk shirt that was open down below his chest, and when he saw Claudia in her short summer dress, stretching up to tie a balloon, well, you can only imagine."

I had never met my father, but I could imagine the scene as though it had been played out in front of me. I knew he and Ergeny, my brother, were like carbon copies, so I could mentally dress him in the white silk shirt, with his toothpaste-commercial smile. Obviously, Fidel would have seemed like a child to my mother, and she probably hadn't given him a second look. She would have been accustomed to young men staring at her, so Fidel would have been just one more. What was more difficult for me to understand was how my mother had fallen so quickly into Ergeny's web, considering he was married to her close friend, Theresa. I could only surmise that he had worked his magic on her, like so many others before, and the fact she was his wife's friend was probably even more of an aphrodisiac than a deterrent. She wasn't a woman of means at that time, and was probably as impressed by the handsome diver who would have brought her gifts that she had never seen before. There was no need to speculate any further. Whatever had happened that made my mother betray her friend and my father betray his wife, had happened, and I was the result.

"Fidel told me once he had only been in love once in his life, and had never fallen out of it. I asked him point blank if he was referring to your mother, and he had bowed his head and nodded, not having the courage or strength to say it out loud."

"What did you tell him?" I was curious as to why she hadn't explained to him that he needed to forget about her forever.

"I told him he needed to follow his heart." I snapped my head up, thinking I must have heard wrong.

"You told him it was okay to see my mother? Are you out of your mind?"

"You think of things in too complicated a manner, sometimes, baby brother." She found a reason to laugh, while I was looking for something to throw against the wall. "You think your mother should be faithful to a man who got her pregnant and then left without a word? And you think your brother Fidel should deny his only love because things get complicated at family reunions?"

I wasn't used to Sandra speaking to me in such a tone of voice. Another breeze brought another nose-full of piggy perfume, and I couldn't help but thinking how I felt exactly how that smelled.

"But why are they sneaking around, hiding?"

"Because they want to be sure it's real, what they both feel, before they sit us all down and bring their relationship out in the open. They're doing it FOR you, not TO you. You're the only person in the world she cares about, and you know Fidel loves you too much to ever hurt you."

I finished the shake, and instinctively picked up the glass to rinse it under the kitchen tap, because I knew too well how the mamey stuck like glue once it had dried. Sandra handed me her own empty glass, thankful for the gesture.

"And what about you?" I felt courageous, suddenly. "When are you going to go after love?"

She had her tongue wedged between her molars, a habit she'd had since childhood – her mother did the same thing. Her shoulders bounced up and down when she laughed, almost like when she danced at the Decada every Friday night behind the Casa de la Musica.

"I did, Michel Ernesto. Three years ago. I gave birth to Aldo and Ariel, and I have everything I want in the world. Now all I want is to see my brothers and sister as happy as I am. What about you? Are you happy?"

"I have everything I've ever asked for."

"That's an easy response, but you didn't answer my question." Sandra stared deep into my eyes, not blinking.

"I really don't know what happiness is, I guess." I hadn't really considered the question to this depth before. "I know I'm not sad, but I don't really know if I'm happy, either." For some reason, I thought about the pretty German girl.

"Do you want your mother to be happy?" She knew the answer to the question, but still posed it, making me say the word out loud.

"Of course, yes. More than anything. She's sacrificed her entire life for me." I was about to stand up, but Sandra pressed my arm back down to a seated position.

"You need to learn to forgive, little brother."

I felt a cold wave spread from my lower back up to the back of my neck. I hadn't come here for this.

"Do you forgive your father?" I said, feeling my throat tightening.

"OUR father, and yes, I did, and I do, and I will, and you know why? Because I don't know what demons he's been fighting all these years. What I do know, though, is I'm not one of them, and neither are Ergeny, or Fidel, or Edith, or you. Something is broken, and we're the only things that have held him together. I'm certain we were on his mind when he jumped from that bridge, as he fell those hundred feet, as he crashed into the river below, and I can only imagine how many broken bones he suffered." She paused for a moment, thinking about the pain our father must have experienced. "Months of recuperation with no one beside him – you were born in that time."

"How did he know about me?" I had been curious since I learned he had taken my name.

"Who else? Vilma, from the bank." He was always in contact with her, sending money regularly. "She never gave up his confidence."

"When he was well enough to, he started moving, using your name in honor of the child he would never know."

I felt the pride I had when Ergeny had shown me the newspaper article.

"I want to talk to Fidel… do you think he'll let me see him?" I needed to change the subject and wanted her permission to try to set things right between us.

"I had hoped you would," she replied, patting my hand and checking in on the boys who would be coming to life any minute. "I asked him to join us for lunch. I hope you're not upset."

I looked at my wise big sister, and just shook my head. At the same time, I felt the catch in my stomach of the nervous energy like I had when I needed to speak in front of the class at school.

"Aldo is awake, and Ariel won't be far behind him," she said, one hand on each side of the bedroom doorway that still only had a thick curtain for a door. "I'm going to prepare their milk. Why don't you unpack your toys for them? They'll be thrilled."

I unpacked the baseball toys, and set them both on the wooden table in the middle of the living room. In a few years, I hoped to replace these plastic toys with real gloves and bats and take them to the local stadium to watch the Gallos play when they came to town for their one and only appearance every year. I tried to remember when the last time was that I'd played a real game of baseball, with balls and gloves and bats. Mostly, my baseball playing had been reduced to swinging a broomstick at a plastic bottle cap in the street in front of the house.

I was left to answer the knock at the door, since Sandra was busy tending to the twins. Fidel was carrying a bag of mangos from the tree in his yard. They were the rare Bizcochuelo mangos from

Santiago de Cuba. Fidel had planted the tree from a seed he'd carried back from a childhood trip. I recognized them from a bag my mother told me she had bought a week earlier. Making the connection now, seeing the same variety of mangos in Fidel's hands, the sweet taste of the mangos I'd devoured came back to me as slightly bitter, framed in another lie.

Fidel had a hopeful smile on his face when I opened the door, looking over my shoulder for Sandra to help take the awkwardness out of the moment. When he didn't see her, he returned his focus to me, and hugged me and kissed my cheek as brothers or family members often do.

"Sandra's in the boys' room," I offered. He looked like he needed an escape route.

"I'll just put these in the kitchen," he said, raising the bag of mangos.

Our brother Ergeny was blessed with the striking good looks, so watching Fidel with his muscular physique sort of surprised me into the realization he was a handsome man in his own right – someone my mother, or any other woman, would be immediately attracted to. Above all else, his gentle nature would endear him to her. As he slipped through the curtain to greet Sandra and the twins, I wondered exactly why it was I had been so upset with the idea of two of the best people I knew in the world being together. Whether I approved or not, though, they were going to be together. They were expecting a baby. A baby brother or sister for me. We'd explain all of the complications when he or she was old enough.

By the time Fidel came back to where I sat flipping through Sandra's extensive collection of music, from Compay Segundo to the Buena Vista Social Club to Pittbull, and everything in between, my heart had softened so much that I stood up and hugged him close to me for a long moment. When I pulled away, I could see both of us were crying – all three of us, in fact – Sandra wiped her eyes with the towel she had in her hand. When either Aldo or Ariel joined in, the three of us switched to laughter, and it was the infectious kind that pulled us from melancholy to festive in just a few minutes. Sandra had prepared a lunch ahead of time of macaroni salad and potatoes stuffed with some sort of fish. She had cut up two avocados and left the seeds in them so they wouldn't turn brown before we got to the table. Her neighbor with the pig had a clandestine soda factory and sold liter bottles to the people on the block at a discount price to pay for their silence. Sandra produced a bottle of pineapple flavor that rivaled any in the shops. Six pesos a bottle was less than a quarter the price of the store-bought drinks. We ate the cool lunch with the soft buns from the bakery near the animal park. I couldn't help but think it would have tasted even better with Edith and Ergeny here to share it with us.

The boys were up and fed and bathed and clothed, and Fidel and I played baseball on the floor with them for nearly an hour before he had to go to the hotel for a scuba lesson. I decided to walk with him to the bus stop and wait with him under the trees there until he found a ride to work. It didn't take long, as a co-worker waved him over to the Jeep he'd found to take him. Fidel gave me a quick squeeze of the shoulder.

"I love you, kid brother," he said as he tossed his pack into the space behind the backseat of the Jeep. I didn't have time to respond before he leapt into the seat, holding the roll-bar for support. I was in no particular hurry, so I watched him until he passed the Cupe gas station and bounced over the rough railway crossing that led to Casilda on the left, and the three beach hotels to the right.

I had one more person to get straight with, and decided that now was as good a time as any. I felt in my pocket for change, and could tell I had enough for a bici-taxi to take me back toward the Barranca. The sun was the enemy at this time of the day – not so much the distance. I spotted a friend from high school who worked the taxi evenings and weekends to help his family, and waved him over. He knew our house from the multiple trips there with tourists, so we chatted about school and mutual friends until he squealed to a stop in front of my house. We played a game of him not wanting to charge me, because I was a friend, and me not wanting to take a free ride from a friend. We both knew I would win, and pay him more than the regular fare, but it was cool he played his role well.

My mother had been cleaning, probably since I'd left early in the morning. I could tell she was nervous when I kissed her cheek. Over her shoulder, I saw the German family sitting in the outdoor garden, enjoying a pitcher of guava juice and some cookies my mother had baked. She must have been extra nervous if she'd baked AND cleaned. The daughter caught me looking at her looking at me, and she turned her attention to some of the flowers near where she was sitting. She was definitely worth a second look.

"Come, sit down, Michel Ernesto... I have something I need to tell you." When she called me by both of my full names, instead of Micho or Honey, I always prepared for something big. Poor thing, I thought, as I followed her into the parlor, as far away from the tourists as was possible. She thinks there might be something she could tell me that would come as a surprise. After the conversations I'd had with my siblings over the past few days, there was very little left that might come as a shock, unless maybe we were really aliens and our mother ship was on its way to pick us up.

"Mom, I know all about Fidel, and how you knew each other before you met my father..." I thought I'd cut her off at the pass, by showing her how much I'd learned in the past twenty-four hours.

She held her hand up to stop me in the middle of my sentence. "I received a phone call an hour ago, just after you'd left Sandra's house." She seemed to be swallowing dry cotton. It was hard for her to get the words out. "It was from your father." Full stop. Did I hear that right? My father? Called my mother?

"What are you talking about? What do you mean, a call from my father? From where? Antartica?"

"He's in Cuba… well, sort of…" She searched my face, wondering if I was ready for the news she was figuring out how to deliver. "He's in jail, in Cienfuegos."

Cienfuegos was the next city to the west, only an hour away from Trinidad. How could my father be in Cienfuegos? How could he be in jail?

"Please explain this to me, Mom." I had my hands tangled in my own hair, my elbows on the table, trying to make my brain work harder than it was capable of.

"You know your father left Cuba illegally, back when he was kidnapped in Colombia?" I nodded. "Well, apparently he called a few weeks ago, offering to turn himself in if they would let him back into Cuba, and let him serve his sentence in Cienfuegos, where we could visit if we want."

"But, excuse me for asking, why did he call YOU?" I could see the slight jab I'd given her, without intending anything bad, had stung. "Sorry, Mom… I don't mean anything by that… I

212

just meant why not Sandra or Ergeny or Theresa..."

She let out a breath through her nostrils, her lips pressed together in a half-smile. "I'm the only one listed on the internet. He found my number before he came back to Cuba."

"Did he tell you anything more? How long is he supposed to be there? Can we see him?" I wanted to rent a car and pick up my brothers and sisters and drive there immediately.

"I called the others. Fidel won't be back from the hotel until late tonight, but Sandra and Ergeny are coming here tomorrow morning, along with our friend Julio Cesar, the lawyer. He told me he'd make some calls today to some friends in Cienfuegos, and try to have more answers when he arrives."

She excused herself when she got emotional again, probably figuring out how he was going to take her pregnancy and relationship with Fidel. I wanted to tell her it didn't matter a grain of salt what he thought about it – she was a free woman. I wanted to tell myself it didn't matter what he thought about me, either. I wanted to, but I couldn't lie to either one of us again today.

The family had finished their drinks and excused themselves to pass by us in the living room, to go to their rooms. I have no idea where the idea came from, but I grabbed the girl's hand as she passed by me, right in front of my mother. I pulled her to me and kissed her full on her perfect German lips.

I was going to meet my father!

FAMILY REUNION

Together at Last

Fidel had arranged with one of the tour bus drivers from the Costa Sur hotel to take all of us to Cienfuegos early Friday morning. We'd pay for the diesel, and give him twenty dollars for his trouble, and we'd have the big van back before the next tour Saturday. The term they liked to use in Cuba for this sort of arrangement was "Socio-lismo", instead of "Socialism" – it meant using your friends, who used the resources available to them for mutually-beneficial purposes. Socios were friends. The prison wouldn't open for visitors until after two in the afternoon, but the driver needed to get there early to deliver some car parts for another socio who was paying him five dollars more. There was more than likely something else heading back to Trinidad that would fetch him another few dollars more, so it would be a good day for him.

For this first visit, the only mother who had chosen to make the journey was Theresa. Claudia had declined for obvious reasons, and Sandra's mother was on husband number four since Ergeny. She had no interest in whether he was alive or dead. Ergeny's mother Lillet had been living in Havana for years, and hadn't even visited her granddaughters in more than two years. Maria, Fidel's mother was busy planning a wedding for her son and Claudia. Technically, Theresa was still Ergeny's wife, although not having seen him in more than ten years would have been plenty enough to justify a divorce had she wanted one. The subject had never come up.

The mood on the bus was somber, nervous. Everyone was dressed in their better clothes, and most had packed extra lunch to leave food with their father. Good food and jail were never used in the same sentence in Cuba. Edith had packed every piece of paper she had ever colored or drawn a picture on to decorate his cell. Ergeny Junior and Fidel sat near the front, chatting with the driver, while Sandra and Ergeny's wife tended to Aldo and Ariel, with the help of Marian and Ines. They discussed the reaction Ergeny would have to seeing his four grandchildren for the first time. They'd probably wait for Fidel to fill him in on the news about the one on the way.

Theresa sat with her head tilted against the window, stroking Edith's braids into place unconsciously. They had passed the bridge over the Cabagan River, where they had celebrated Edith's sixteenth birthday not so long ago. She watched the landmarks tick by – the shrimp farm where a giant shrimp sculpture was enough to scare anyone from eating the horrific creatures – the big indian at the entrance to the Gaujimico Villa where Claudia had invited them to swim in the big pool a few years earlier – the giant tree that towered over the highway at the junction to some other small community to the south she had never been to. She still marveled at the beach that had been formed a few years earlier by Hurricane Dennis when it had pounded the city and area for two days. From bad came something beautiful. The river at Cabagan had changed its course, too, draining into the ocean from the opposite side of the bridge. Nature was so powerful.

Michel Ernesto kept to himself. Everyone had different emotions and internal issues to wrestle with on their way to see the ghost that was Ergeny. Finally, after ten years as a moving target, their father was somewhere he couldn't run from.

The van slowed to almost a stop where they turned left near the giant cement factory, signaling they were about fifteen minutes from Cienfuegos, the Pearl of the South, as it was known. It was a beautiful city, with wide streets and plenty of clean restaurants and museums. Punta Gorda had a big old yacht club that had been restored to its previous glory, and there was a rich tradition of live music and cabaret shows at the Jagua Hotel at the end of the Paseo el Prado, where the classic cars made constant loops to provide transportation and to just show off.

They wouldn't see much of the city this time, though. They would skirt around it on the east side, passing by the twin fourteen story apartment buildings in Reparto Pastora, and taking the second exit of the large traffic circle to head toward Aguada and the autopista highway to Havana. The prison was located about ten minutes to the north of the city.

The driver left the family at the entrance to the prison, about a half kilometer from the main gates. He didn't have authorization to drive in any closer, so he agreed to pick them up at the same place a few hours later, when visiting hours were over. Julio Cesar had pulled some serious strings in order to get authorization for ten visitors on the same day. Visits were normally limited to immediate family, but in this case, he convinced them that this was, in fact, immediate family, or families, as it were.

There had been arrangements for a special room for the extraordinary visit, due to the size of the family, and not wanting other inmates to see the exceptional situation that might set new precedents. There was also a question of special access they had to deal with in Ergeny's case.

When the guard in charge of the visits saw the gang converging on the entrance, he rushed over to herd them toward an annex used for training, where they could meet without being seen by the general population. Ergeny Junior and Fidel produced the copy of the authorization Julio Cesar had printed for them, and they filed each of the others past, checking off their names from the list on the sheet as they went through. Someone else inspected their bags of food and personal effects. Ergeny had forgotten to leave his knife at home, so the guard would hold it until he left. Soda cans were also contraband, so the inspector had two cola drinks for later in his shift, thanks to Michel Ernesto.

Once settled into the training room, the guard gave them a brief but serious speech about the rules of engagement, mostly referring to the conduct expected of the minors. Fidel checked his watch and signaled with his finger toward his wrist that it was already two fifteen, and visiting hours were short enough for one person, let alone ten of them. The guard was in a good mood, and smiled at the gesture, which on a bad day might have cancelled the visit altogether, just to remind the visitor who was in charge. He must have had grandchildren himself, given his age. He excused himself to retrieve the prisoner from where he was waiting.

Ergeny had shown the most recent pictures he'd found in his research to everyone in the group. They were from Argentina, about two years earlier. Senior's hair had morphed from black with a few flecks of grey to grey with a few reminders of black. His face was still as handsome, though. Edith found space on a training table to begin sorting her impressive collection of school drawings and report cards she wanted to show off to her father, and had even found a roll of packing tape he could use to attach them to his walls.

Sandra had suggested an informal schedule for the visit – first, they would all meet with him together, and for the second half of the visiting hours, each child would have ten minutes alone with him to speak privately. She would begin, and they would continue in order. They set chairs in a semi-circle so everybody would have equal access at first. They were allowed a brief hug when the visit began, and a brief hug when time was up.

They were still busy rearranging furniture when the door opened, stopping them in their tracks. They had been expecting him to come in through the door the guard had left by, but he surprised them by entering from another door behind them. As they collectively turned, they were greeted by the unwavering movie star smile of Ergeny Senior – in a wheelchair.

Ergeny Junior could have used his trusty knife to cut through the silence of that first shocking moment. The guard pushed the chair with its wobbly front wheel into the room, and returned to lock the door with a key. He sat on a wooden chair beside the door to take in the spectacle.

Sandra moved first, somehow breaking through the invisible boundary that had held ten people motionless. She asked with her eyes if she could hug him, and he offered his lap with a smile, tears streaming down his face as he surveyed the group, trying to erase eleven years of distance. She sobbed uncontrollably as her father did his best to console her, touching her short hair and wiping her tears with his other hand. The flood gates opened, and nine more bodies converged on the wheelchair, until the guard cleared his throat loudly. They knew the rules.

Sandra decided to be the moderator of the event, and asked everyone to take a seat, placing Ergeny Senior in the center of the semi-circular arrangement.

"Dad, we all have a hundred things we want to say to you and ask you, but I think it's important that we get a few introductions out of the way. There are some of us whom you haven't met, yet, and it's long overdue. She called Michel Ernesto to join her in the middle, beside their father. "This amazing and handsome young man is Michel Ernesto."

There was a pause, while Ergeny examined him from top to bottom. "It's a pleasure to finally meet you, Michel Ernesto. I know you know I'm a big fan of your name." That brought a welcome laugh from the group, and erased a lot of the tension in the room.

"It's good to finally meet you, too, Dad." Michel Ernesto was overcome by his emotion at finally being able to call someone 'dad', and he reached for Sandra and buried his head into her shoulder. Ergeny Senior was just close enough to reach over and touch his son's arm from behind.

Sandra called Ergeny Junior's two daughters next. "This one, Marion, is your first grandchild." She handed Marion to her grandfather, who accepted a kiss on the cheek and a quick hug around the neck. "And this beautiful thing is Ines, your second grandchild." Ergeny Junior prodded Ines to give her grandfather a kiss like her sister had, but she hid behind his chair and refused to even look at him. "And finally, these two boys, Aldo and Ariel, are numbers three and four." The boys were more interested in the wheelchair than in the strange man in it. "The rest of us you know, but as you can see, your little princess Edith is now a big, beautiful girl."

Edith couldn't contain herself, and threw herself into Ergeny's arms, forcing the chair back and to one side. He was in a wheelchair, but to Edith he could still leap tall buildings. Unwavering love was a beautiful thing to watch, and even the guard was touched by the sobs of joy coming from the sweet girl. Ergeny Senior had maintained his composure very well up to that point, considering the emotional hurricane he must have been experiencing. Edith pushed him over the edge, though, and he held her tight to his chest and almost screamed into her shoulder and neck. Fathers and daughters. Theresa hadn't moved from her spot at the end of the row of chairs. She wanted to let the children and grandchildren have their time. Seeing the spectacle of her daughter with her father, the two of them holding onto each other for dear life, brought her to her knees, holding her face in her hands.

"You all want to know why I'm in this contraption," he finally spoke, when he felt he could get words out. Nodding heads and spoken agreement. "I had some wonderful doctors patch me up after I jumped from the bridge in Colombia." Edith hadn't left her spot on his lap, and wiped his cheeks tenderly as he spoke. "The river wasn't quite deep enough, and I couldn't stop myself before I hit the bottom, feet first. I crushed four vertebrae, and two ribs punctured my right lung. It took several hours to get me to a hospital, and weeks before I even came back to consciousness. That was probably what saved me – I hadn't moved since they pulled me out of the river, two miles from where I'd gone in. Somehow, the nerves had survived the broken bones, and after a few more months of physiotherapy, I was able to walk again, but with two canes.

Ergeny Junior broke in. "But I have pictures of you in Bolivia, winning a fishing derby, less than a year later."

Senior smiled at his mirror image. "I walked with a cane, but I dove with a spear gun. I had a brace made, and could dive almost as well as ever before. It was on land that I failed. They started to call me 'the sea turtle' behind my back, because

I was slow and awkward on land, but no one could catch me in the water."

"And now? The wheelchair?"

"Time caught up to me, finally. I got too confident, walked too much, until finally canes and crutches weren't enough."

Fidel couldn't wait for his private visit. "Isn't anyone going to ask? Why did you leave? Without a word to anyone?"

Senior adjusted Edith on his lap. "Fair question, Fidel. No good answer, though... I wanted to end my vicious cycle of doing what you all know I'd been for far too long." Edith turned to look him in the eyes, waiting for him to say it out loud. Michel Ernesto bowed his head. People turned to look for Theresa's reaction, but found none.

"I don't think running away was a solution," Junior joined in. "Look around... look at all of the lives you left in limbo." He stared at the face of the man who had denied on the street that he was his father. "Look at my daughters."

Theresa could maintain her silence no longer.

"Enough, everybody. Your father came back from freedom to this place, just so he could be close to all of you. Don't question it. Just enjoy it." Then, when they thought she'd finished, she turned her attention to Senior. "And how much longer are you going to continue to hide and deny what happened to you?"

Senior looked like he'd been shot in the chest. He'd guarded his secret all his life, never sharing a single detail with anyone, not even Theresa.

"You're not the first child in the world to have been abused by his father. It's nothing you did wrong and nothing to be ashamed of."

Now the rest of the siblings stared at Theresa in shock. They'd never heard anything of the sort.

"Why do all of you think he left before you were old enough to remember? Your father was sexually and physically abused by his father when he was just a little boy. He left every one of his wives because he was afraid he'd do the same to his own children."

Sandra wanted to silence Theresa, but knew what she was hearing made sense, somehow. She searched her father's face for denial, but found the opposite. He looked defeated, spent.

"There's no point anymore… what's done is done," Senior replied. Edith reached up again and wrapped her arms around his neck.

Sandra decided it was time for the private meetings, and asked Edith if she'd mind joining her mother for a few minutes. Reluctantly, Edith climbed down and returned to her mother. Sandra could see the look of anxiety on Edith's face…

even this separation from her father was traumatic. She called her back to show her pictures to Senior as she wheeled him to the private visit corner of the room. That was all it took to bring Edith back to the present, proudly pointing out all of the pictures of the three of them – the mother in some of the pictures with dark skin, the father with white skin, and the little girl somewhere in between. They ranged from stick people at her earliest school age to elaborate landscapes, usually including the ocean and fish, but always with the three of them together. Senior picked up each one in turn, and seemed to scan it to memory, shaking his head all the while. By the time he picked up the last in the series, his hands trembled from his emotions. Edith smiled with pride with every gesture from her father that he liked one more than the previous. Finally, Sandra wheeled her father over to the most remote area of the room. The guard quietly joined them, to ensure they weren't plotting an elaborate escape.

"Sandra, you look fantastic," was the first thing Senior could manage. "And your boys are amazing." The boys were still more interested in the wheelchair than their grandfather. "I'm sorry, but I can't tell which is which."

"Aldo is more like you – he cries when I try to take him out of the water – and Ariel is another Fidel. He's quiet and thoughtful. Aldo is a little devil, always taking his brother's toys, just to leave them a minute later." Sandra paused, realizing she was describing her own father even more than she meant to. "Sorry, I didn't mean…" Senior laughed out loud for the first time since they had seen him, finding his old sense of humor.

"You'll want to get Aldo into therapy soon, then!" Senior quipped. Sandra relaxed, thinking she might have offended her father unintentionally.

"I know everybody is going to ask you the same question, but I need to ask it anyway." Senior turned the chair to face her head on, ready for the obvious. "Why didn't you contact us? Why did you run away for so many years? And why did you come back, after all this time?"

"That's a lot of questions at one time for an old man, but I'll try." Sandra found a chair and sat down, to face him at his own level. The boys looked like they wanted to play somewhere else, so she signaled to Theresa with her eyes, and she called them to join her and Edith. "I left because I felt like I couldn't continue the cycle any more, leaving children without fathers as I had too many times already, and then, with Claudia telling me she was keeping her baby, I couldn't face it even one more time – falling in love with someone who I was going to leave."

Sandra's face showed the question. He continued. "Theresa knows things… I don't know how, and what you heard a few minutes ago has a lot to do with what you're asking me with your look. I left because I couldn't bear to find out if I was like my old man."

"So you were abused by your father, my grandfather?" Sandra's heart sank in her chest at the thought.

"I've never spoken to anyone about it, but he started when I was four years old, or at least that's when I remember. That's why I had to leave before any of you were as old as I was at the time."

"But you've never felt the urge to abuse a child…" Sandra glanced over at her own two boys, playing with Edith. "You're not your father."

"I've never imagined hurting any child, ever. But I didn't know what was wrong with my father, either, because as far as I know he never touched anyone but his own children."

Sandra looked at her father like she was seeing him for the first time. So much suffering inside. She thought back to all of the things her mother had said about him over the years. And all of the things she had heard on the street.

"What about your mother?" Sandra asked him. "Didn't she do anything to stop him?"

"My mother knew what he was doing. She punished me for it. She let him do what he wanted, as long as there was money for food and clothing every month."

"Does that have something to do with your obsession with women?"

"I wish I could understand that myself," he responded quietly. "I've been with so many women, and loved so few of them."

Sandra paused again, not knowing if she wanted to know the answer.

"And my mother? Did you love her?"

"I really thought I did, but we were kids, your mother and me. Playing house."

"Do you love anyone, now?" That question stopped Senior from continuing. Sandra watched his expression change from an old man to a hopeful teenager. He couldn't form the words.

"Theresa?" Sandra asked, looking over his shoulder to where Theresa played with Edith and her twins. Her father's expression told her the answer. She wondered what the chances were.

When she looked at her watch, she realized she had already passed her private time, and decided there were others who were just as anxious as she had been for answers. She had gotten some, and they had generated more questions, but there would be time to get more answers on other occasions. She kissed her father on the forehead, her hands framing his face, and signaled to Junior that it was his turn. Senior put his hands over hers, and winked at her, like he had when she was a little girl. Sandra stepped back and gave him a thumbs up, which he returned to her with both thumbs, a tear following a wrinkle that passed through his deep dimple.

Junior held Ines in his arms, and guided Marian to the chair in front of her grandfather. Marian carried a small box, wrapped with a ribbon that looked like it came from her hair.

"Dad, I'm glad you're here, and safe," Junior started.

"I've gone back to my original first name, Son." Senior hoped to see a sign of forgiveness from the son he had denied so many years ago.

Junior chuckled. "You don't look much like a Michel Ernesto."

"I heard it was you who found me in South America. You even called the lady who owned the house where I rented a room. You just missed me by a few minutes, but didn't leave a number."

"Would you have called?" Junior hadn't truly torn down the walls that had been built between them over the years.

"I wanted to call. To congratulate you for your daughters. "You know that Vilma kept me informed."

"Yes, I know. She should be a spy, that one. She never gave up a single clue, even when I tried to pressure her."

"She's been a good friend... the mother I wish I'd had."

"But you could have been here with us, to congratulate me in person... to throw the girls up in the air and catch them." That struck a nerve in Senior, whose eyes welled up with tears.

"I thought about that every day, Ergeny... believe me. But what if I..."

"Dad, I have never once had the slightest urge to hurt my daughters, or my nephews or anyone else. And I'm happy with my wife and family. We don't have to turn into our fathers. I'm human, and I'm a man, and I won't say that I've been the perfect husband. I've taken the things that have been offered to me over the years, but I always came home to my family. That's why I searched for you all these years. I think I'm the only one of us who really knew you were capable of surviving that fall from the bridge. We share the same genes." Ironically, Junior felt a shortage of breath, suddenly, and asked Fidel to toss him one of his bottles of ice water. He took a long drink, and it occurred to him to pass the bottle to his father, who held it in just the same way, drinking the last of the water, leaving only a chunk of ice for later.

"Funny," Senior said, looking at the green bottle. "I used to drink out of a bottle just like this one."

"Not JUST like this one," Junior replied, taking it back from his father."

Senior looked at him, incredulous. "I guess I didn't leave you much when I left, did I?"

"That bottle has come and gone with me to the ocean hundreds of times, and I've never died of thirst, so I guess it was as good a gift as most." He smiled his father's smile, and looked over at Marian. "Why don't you give your grandpa his gift, now?"

Marian picked up the box and carried it, arms outstretched, to where Senior took it from her, and accepted another kiss on the cheek. Seeing how she stared at the ribbon, he signaled for her to help him to open the box. She smiled and eagerly untied the bow, keeping the ribbon for herself. Together, they pulled the top off of the little box, revealing the collar with the three barracuda teeth. Between each of the teeth, Junior had added two shark's teeth. "I'll tell you the story sometime," Junior said, when he saw the look on his father's face as he held it in his hands after so many years.

Sandra had been watching from the other side of the room, waiting for this moment. She'd helped him to have the shark's teeth added, from the same friend who had made the original. The clasp had also been removed and replaced with a better one. She ran her hand through her short hair, caught in the emotion of seeing the treasure returned to its rightful owner after so long.

Junior unbuttoned his own shirt, revealing a similar chain, decorated with teeth from the same shark.

"I'd like that," was all Senior could manage to say. He signaled for Marian to help him put the chain around his neck, and breathed a sigh when he felt it in place again, finally.

"I think our time's up, for today." Junior signaled for Marian to give her grandfather a hug, and handed Ines to Senior to do the same.

"Are we good, you and I?" Senior asked, quietly.

"We're good, Dad. As long as you promise to watch your granddaughters grow up."

"I was always so afraid I'd fall into the same hole with my grandchildren... never sure. Now..." He signaled to the chair, and below his waist. "Now there's no question anymore."

Junior was sad to acknowledge his father's handicap, but nodded his head in understanding. "Well, from the entrance to my little finca you can see the Batea." He and his father hugged for the first time in nearly thirty years, and it was just as difficult for each of them to separate. Junior gathered both his daughters into his strong arms, and carried them to where the rest of the group waited. He nodded to Fidel to go to his father, and felt the need to bury his head in Sandra's shoulder, crying like a baby.

Fidel had something he needed to tell his father, and knew it wouldn't be easy. He felt like he had betrayed him, and wondered if he would have given up Claudia altogether had she not been expecting his baby, given the news his father was indeed alive.

"Fidel, my sweet and gentle son," Ergeny started, asking with his hands for Fidel to pull his chair up close. "You know Vilma has been my very dear friend for all these years."

Fidel nodded, knowing as everyone did this was true.

"She tells me things she feels I need to know."

Now Fidel looked at him with a question mark formed by his eye brows.

"You have my blessing... both of you. You have my support one hundred percent."

"You know about Claudia and me?" Fidel exhaled as though he'd been twenty meters deep in the ocean since he'd sat down in front of his father.

"And I know about the baby, too. I couldn't be happier for both of you." Fidel had his hands plastered to his face, covering his eyes, hearing the words he'd needed to for so many years.

"I never wanted to betray you, even when I thought you were dead."

"I've asked Vilma about you so many times over the years she didn't want to hear it anymore. I just wanted to know you were happy."

"As of this very moment, I think I finally am. I love her so much, Dad…"

"Then do me a favor… marry the woman and never leave her! You both deserve it. And Michel Ernesto, too. He needs a father around the house."

Fidel looked at his father for a long moment. "Then you'll have to visit us a lot. YOU'RE his father. I'm his brother. He needs YOU around him." They looked over at Michel Ernesto, and Fidel waved him over, out of turn. Sandra smiled her understanding.

Michel Ernesto came over, almost reluctantly, not wanting to interrupt Fidel's time. Senior signaled for his youngest son to pull up another chair beside Fidel's.

"Son," he said, looking at Michel Ernesto, taking in every feature of the man in front of him. "I want you to know that I am sorry for what I did to your mother and to you, leaving the way I did."

Michel Ernesto looked away, staring at the cracks in the paint of the wall beside him. They looked like branches on a crooked tree.

"Can I tell you how much I always hated you?" Michel Ernesto said to him, turning his head to look straight into Senior's eyes. "That I didn't cry at your funeral? That I was called a bastard all my life?"

Senior melted into his chair, looking older than his actual age. "Yes, Son... you can tell me everything you want or need to. I know I hurt your mother very badly, and obviously you, too. I know I hurt everybody in this room. That's why I'm here. In this prison. I want to spend the rest of my days trying to make up for all of those things."

Michel Ernesto's sudden outburst had grabbed the attention of everyone in the room, including the guard, who had gotten to his feet, in case there was more aggression. As usual, Michel Ernesto stood up, searching for an escape route. "Can you let me out of here?" he said to the guard.

"You've only got another fifteen minutes, and then all of you have to leave," he responded.

Michel Ernesto saw the look in Fidel's eyes, pleading for him to sit back down and talk to his father.

"You don't need to feel bad about hating me, Michel Ernesto... I hate myself more than you ever could, believe me. When I look at you I'm reminded of how many moments I've missed in so many lives. I have a grown child that I've never met until today, a baby girl who's a grown woman already, and grandchildren..."

"How long are you going to be here, anyway?" Michel Ernesto had sat back down in his chair, but still had an attitude of antagonism.

"If I don't get into any trouble, I'll be out in eighteen months, maybe even less." He signaled to the wheelchair. "They don't think I'm going to run anywhere anymore."

"They don't know you like we do," Michel Ernesto couldn't help but get in one final barb.

For some reason, the image made Senior laugh, and Fidel joined in, until Michel Ernesto couldn't help but be infected, too. The three of them laughed so hard that it made the guard laugh, and then the children came running to see what was so funny.

"I can just see him... racing down that road to the highway, with the front wheel wobbling a million miles an hour..." Michel Ernesto's anger had turned to unbridled joy. They laughed until it was no longer funny, and then laughed a little more. The three of them looked like they'd run a hundred yard dash by the time they stopped coughing and caught their breath.

When they were settled again, Senior asked Fidel to show him his hands once more. Fidel obliged, not knowing what his father intended. After examining both hands, he pointed to the index finger on Fidel's right hand. "That's where your first prawn got you, isn't it?"

Fidel looked at his father incredulously. "Yes, right there." He pointed to the half-inch-long scar.

"I went in the first time with my left hand," Senior said, showing his own scar, among many more. They were so old that they almost blended in with his thick, calloused skin, now all-the-worse from manipulating the old wheelchair.

"We still have the scar you left in our front door the night you left," Michel Ernesto pointed out. "My mother chose never to fix it."

"We can fix it together, the three of us," Fidel decided. "In about eighteen months. There'll be another grandchild to get to know then.

The guard motioned that time was running out for the visit, so they hurried to let Edith and Theresa have their turn. Edith had gathered up all of the papers and the tape, and placed them carefully in a plastic bag. Theresa had packed a half loaf of bread, and carried a fresh tomato, avocado, and a little bag of salt, and carried them over to prepare them fresh for Senior. She realized when she spread them on the small table-top that she didn't have a knife to cut the tomato or avocado. She looked over at the guard, who smiled, and pulled out the knife he'd been holding for Junior.

"To be safe, I'd better do it myself," he said, reaching for the tomato. He sliced it onto the bread, and made a quick cut around the seed of the avocado. "Did you bring these from Trinidad?" he asked Theresa, as he popped the large avocado into two pieces, revealing the bright yellow meat inside. "I haven't seen one this nice here in Cienfuegos."

"It's from our own tree," piped in Edith, eager to help finish the sandwich for her father. "I'll put the salt on." She bit a little hole in the corner of the tiny bag of salt, and expertly distributed it around the sandwich, sure she had done it just like her mother had explained on the way. Senior sat back, a smile on his face, watching his daughter prepare the meal that had been so much a part of his life. The pride on his face couldn't have been hidden with a mask.

"First things, first," he said, when she handed it to him. He took a large bite and chewed it as though it was the finest steak in the best restaurant. Theresa had already produced the bottle of ice water, and he tipped it up and took a long drink from it. Then he offered the sandwich to Edith. "Take a bite of this," he said, and you'll know why your mother is the best person in the entire world. Edith tried to match the size of her father's bite, but fell a little short. She handed it to her mother, who also took a small bite. The two of them drank from the same water bottle, and Theresa felt like it was time to say what needed saying.

"Remember the day I told you that your father had forgiven you?" she said.

"I remember it every day of my life," Senior responded, setting the water bottle down beside his chair.

"Well, there are two more people YOU need to forgive, before you can get on with your life."

Senior looked at her, waiting for her to explain. Surely she didn't mean her and Edith.

"You need to forgive your father," she continued. Senior took a deep breath, involuntarily, filling his chest cavity with enough air for a deep dive into shark-infested water.

"But my father doesn't deserve anyone's forgiveness."

"It's not for your father's benefit," she explained, pulling Edith tight to her side. "It's for yours... and hers."

Senior looked at the floor, then over toward the rest of his extended family, who were all watching in silence. "I've never considered forgiving him. I blamed him for making me into the animal I've always been."

"Well, I'm here to tell you life is too short, and there are a bunch of people who need you to be in a better place in your heart." She brushed her hand in an arc, indicating the children and grandchildren in the room. Then she turned her eyes down to the perfect braids of her daughter's head. "This one needs her hero to be whole again. Those tall buildings aren't going to leap themselves."

Senior grinned at the thought. He certainly never considered himself capable of being anyone's hero, but the way that perfect little face looked at him, he could tell she saw him as a lot more than he did himself.

"I'll try, really I will. I'll spend time with the padre who visits us here, and see if we can work something out."

"Good, then there's just one more person left to forgive. You can talk to the padre about him, too."

Senior reached down for the water, feeling suddenly dry and uncomfortable.

"Myself, right?"

Theresa nodded, offering the sandwich to him again. When he reached for it, she grabbed his hand in hers, and squeezed it, tightly.

"And when you're finished paying your dues in here, if you've done what I told you, there's a little old house in the Barranca waiting for you."

Senior's lips quivered and he let out the air he'd been holding in his lungs. He reached for the handkerchief in his pocket to wipe his tears, and squeezed Theresa's hand back.

"You would really take me back into your home?" he said, incredulously, "After what I did?"

"First of all, it's not my home, it's OUR home. Always has been. No other man has ever spent a night in our bed, and I don't have any plans for any other but you to do so anytime soon."

Senior's face took on a defeated look, as he once again looked down at himself, and back up at Theresa, who knew exactly what he was thinking.

"Don't you worry about such things, Old Man. Just plan to clean up after yourself, and that'll be enough. At least I won't worry about you chasing after another skirt."

"Theresa, it's been so long. Do you think we can really be a family again?"

"Don't ask me... ask her," Theresa responded, looking down at Edith, who was pulling at her mother's arm to let her escape into her father's embrace. "She'll be the judge and jury."

"I'm so sorry about the day I left... it wasn't right, and it wasn't fair to you."

"Every time you left to go to the ocean, I wondered if you would come back. I worried about sharks, and barracudas, and everything else out there that could keep you from returning. But you came back, every time. Some of those times you smelled more like rum or some other woman than you did the ocean, but what was I to expect? This time, you came back later than usual, but I don't smell rum or perfume on you, so that's a bonus." She smiled at him, and he knew he had a place to go home to, and that would sustain him for however many months it would take to get there.

The guard advised them that they had already overstayed their time, so he would need to get them out of there quickly. Theresa wrapped the unused avocado in the plastic bag, and handed it to him, promising to bring him more the following week. The rest of the care packages were gathered into a larger bag, and tied onto the handle of the wheelchair.

One by one, as they had done when they arrived, each of the family filed past the guard to hug Senior goodbye. He was as happy as he could remember being, and as sad as he could remember being, all at the same time.

Edith had the hardest time of all, holding the door with both hands so the guard couldn't close it. He finally allowed her one extra hug, and she agreed to let him close it.

The bus-ride home was very different from the one to Cienfuegos. Everyone seemed to have something to say about how their father looked, what he'd said to them, things they wanted to send for him to eat. Sandra settled in beside Theresa after the twins had fallen asleep. She took her hands and held them to her face, kissing her fingers. Theresa looked content, but not ecstatic, like she'd just been waiting for her husband to come home from a fishing trip, and it had taken eleven years for him to return. What was another eighteen months?

Edith talked non-stop to Michel Ernesto, who looked like a different person from the one who had stared out the window the entire trip earlier in the day. She wanted his help to decorate their house for the party when her father came home. He smiled at the idea.

Fidel and Ergeny sat together near the front of the van, each holding a sleeping girl.

"Should we bring the monument back up?" Fidel asked.

"No, I think it's just fine where it is. He still lives there, whether or not he'll be able to ever see it." They agreed there was no reason to disturb the reef. A dozen fish called it home.

Theresa never missed a visit, and never failed to bring something special for Senior and the guard to enjoy. She carried the things other family members wanted to send, and brought back letters to all of them from their father. Some weeks, one of the children joined her, but mostly she went alone. The faithful wife.

Lack of conditions for a physically-challenged person was the pretext for reducing his sentence to six months from eighteen, and there was a resounding cheer from the other inmates when they saw him packing his drawings to go home. He'd endeared himself to everyone there with his endless stories of exploits above and below the surface of the ocean.

He'd asked Theresa to bring a bag of her special avocados as a gift to the others, and Fidel had sent a large bag of the special mangos from his tree as well. The prisoners would enjoy a feast thanks to the diver that night.

Michel Ernesto and Claudia had pulled out all the stops for the welcome-home party, even though she was so big she could hardly walk. The street in front of the little house in the Barranca was decorated with balloons and banners and flowers and she'd even arranged for a giant barracuda piñata for the kids, filled with sweets and pencils and erasers and little plastic toys. Sandra had a friend from the Candonga who played in a musical group, and they were setting up their equipment when the car horns began to sound from the main street, four blocks away. Theresa had been cooking all morning, and Edith had made a big banner for the entrance to the house with lots of flowers and suns and stars on it. It said, simply, 'Welcome home, Daddy'.

Fidel and Ergeny had rented a car and driver to bring him home in style, with air conditioning and everything.

Michel Ernesto inspected his gift to his father. The concrete appeared to be dry enough, so he used an old hammer to pull the footings off of the wheelchair ramp that led to the doorway. He would have it tiled the following week.

Claudia had hired the best welders in town to build a wheelchair accessible tricycle so that he could get around the small city on his own, to visit children and grandchildren.

The honks became louder and more frequent, and were obviously not from just one car. When they rounded the corner, the welcome party was amazed to see an entire train of cars, led by the shiny red convertible of Chichi, who had propped Ergeny Senior onto the open back seat, parading him around the city like a girl celebrating her fifteenth birthday. Fidel and Ergeny Junior followed close behind them, and faces that hadn't

246

been seen for years piled out of the other vehicles and bicycles and even two carretons had joined the parade.

The music started up, and the neighbors carried pots of beans and rice and vegetables to the makeshift table in the street. The smell of the pig roasting in the backyard wafted over the clay rooftops. The beer truck parked itself down the street, and had a steady stream of customers. They were all surprised to have their pesos refused – Claudia had purchased the entire tank for the party. Coolers of the homemade soda were supplied by Sandra and her neighbor, and Chichi surprised everyone when he opened his trunk to reveal a big sack of fresh lobsters. He jokingly said they'd been left over from Senior's funeral.

The most emotional part of the day for Senior, though, was when Edith presented him with the two pictures of his five children and his five wives. In the background, he could see the dozens of fishing boats and recognized the Batea immediately.

The delegate from the CDR who had sanctioned the party, had to send everyone home after complaints from several blocks away of the music and noise. It was after four in the morning by the time Chichi wheeled his big red Chevrolet back toward his house at La Boca. Theresa surveyed the street and decided it was best to worry about it in the morning. She smiled up at the big teeth hanging from the empty barracuda, still dangling from the thick twine between her house and the Oliviera's across the street. Corbatica had kept the children entertained for hours with his silliness. He had to have been in his sixties, she estimated, since he'd entertained her when she was a little girl. It was definitely time he got some new material, though, she chuckled to herself. "Tacita tacita tacita," she mimicked him, clicking her fingertips together as he always did to start his show.

Inside the house, she picked up a few glasses and plates that had been set on any horizontal surface. There hadn't been enough pork left to even make a sandwich for breakfast. They'd sent a bici-taxi to the bakery across from the little zoo twice for more buns. Sandra's neighbor had sent two extra cases of soda for the kids, and somebody's relative worked at the ice factory, and sent an entire slab in a carreton. People would remember this party for years, she was sure.

She stopped in mid-step when she saw Senior sprawled on the bed, fully-clothed, with Edith asleep on his chest. She'd tried to send her home with Claudia and Michel Ernesto, but she'd refused to leave her father's side, even for a minute.

It had probably been a good thing, too, since Claudia's water broke on the way home, and she and Fidel were on their way to Sancti Spiritus by ambulance at this very moment. Sandra would follow with Ergeny when they could arrange for a car in the morning. Quite the party, she thought to herself, continuing to the kitchen to make her little house her own again. She looked over at the little bathroom – the workers were coming in a few hours to make it accessible.

The best builders in Trinidad would be busy for the next couple of weeks, making five houses accessible to the wheelchair-bound father who had returned from the dead. Junior, ever the inventor, had a ramp installed from the highway down to his house, with a pulley system that allowed his father to connect the chair to a hook that would pull him up the steep hill and would keep him from going too fast on the way back down. He had built a flat area at the top, with a thatched roof, where Senior could sit and watch the ocean for as long as he wanted. He had found an old telescope that would bring the Batea so close it felt like a person could reach into the water.   In case his father was watching, Junior would give a big thumbs up before stepping into the water with his spear for a day of fishing.

Senior spent his days visiting each of his children, and helping to clean the fish Junior brought home. It was one of the things he felt he could do to earn his keep, now that he wasn't able-bodied anymore.

At the table at the little finca, his granddaughters always asked the two men to swap stories. One of their favorites was the day their grandfather had been left in the ocean by the government fishing boat. They had miscounted the crew and were ten minutes away by the time someone realized he wasn't on board. When the boat arrived, someone counted more than two hundred shark fins, circling around him. When he was in a serious mood, Senior would tell them about the terror he had felt, knowing that the movement of his fins and hands in the water was what was drawing them closer and closer, and a couple of them had already rubbed up against him, preparing their attack, by the time the boat came to his rescue. When he felt more jovial, he told them that the only thing that scared him more was the thought of his five wives being together at the Batea.

Junior told them about the time he'd been inches away from a three meter white shark that had attacked the lobster trap he was preparing to harvest, and how he'd tossed the big lobster from his hand, just as the shark planned to take it from him, forearm and all. The two Ergenys shared scars from barracudas, lobster and prawns.

Senior produced pictures they had taken of the giant devil ray he had harpooned months before he'd left Cuba. It had taken him and his buddy on a three hour tour, like the song from 'Gilligan's Island', before he'd gotten close enough to stab it while his partner jumped into the water to sink another hook into it. When he came out of the blood-soaked water, Senior decided it was time to show him the dozens of sharks that had come for the feast. They'd tossed pieces to the sharks to keep them at bay while they cut the wings off to bring them back. The tail itself had been over four meters long, and the two wings weighed more than four hundred pounds. They'd run out of gas coming back from open sea where it had pulled them, and had finally been towed in by a military patrol boat.

Most days, though, he was content to take Edith and Michel Ernesto to school, and play with his latest grandson, Ernesto. They'd named him in honor of his older brother, and because that was the name of Fidel's best friend, Che Guevara. Fidel and Che, together again, they'd said when they announced his name when they returned from Sancti Spiritus a few days after the party.

On the fifth anniversary of his 'death', Fidel and Junior had come up with a special surprise for their father. Chichi was involved in the plan, too. Sandra had been against it, at first, worried about their father. Michel Ernesto had connections in some high-up places, and got involved right from the start. They filled Theresa and Edith in on the plan from the beginning, to make sure they were on board.

The morning of the anniversary date came around, and Senior was informed they were meeting at Ergeny's ranch for a commemorative meal. He thought it was a little strange Theresa had prepared his traditional lunch of a tomato and avocado sandwich and three bottles of water, but she was always prepared, he assumed.

Chichi had picked them up in his convertible, and insisted Senior ride on the back again, with Edith by his side. Claudia and little Che rode up front, and Theresa and Sandra and the twins sat in the back seat. The music was Polo Montanez' first and most-loved album, 'Guajiro Natural', blaring from six big speakers as they paraded through La Boca on the way to Ergeny's finca. The Captain's house still pulled at Senior's heart when they drove past it. He waited for Chichi to slow the big car down to turn into Junior's place, but he continued past it. That's when they saw the armada of fishing boats once again anchored outside the Batea, and the strangest-looking contraption Senior had ever seen. A giant wheel, ten feet in diameter and four feet wide, was sitting next to the highway. It wasn't until they hauled his wheelchair out of the trunk and placed it inside the wheel that Senior caught on to the elaborate plan. He was too heavy to carry the hundred yards to the water, and his wheelchair couldn't be pushed through the soft sand or over the sharp rocks of the shore, so they'd made him a wheelchair access like no other. When they got him into the chair, two men began to roll the wheel toward the water, where Michel Ernesto was backing into the little bay with a magnificent tour boat complete with a glass bottom. The wheel worked to perfection, and kept Sandra and Theresa busy wheeling Senior along inside it as it approached the edge of the water. Leaving the soft sand and crackling over the porous surface of the lava rock bounced them about for a few seconds, causing Edith to yelp with joy, perched on her father's lap for the ride. Four fishermen produced another invention for the event – four big truck tire tubes had been filled with air and strapped together, with a sheet of thick plywood fastened to the top, just long enough to protrude from each end of the tubes to form a natural ramp. They held it firmly against the rough edge of the rocks so that he could be wheeled onto it where the brakes were set. Michel Ernesto, already in his diving suit, tugged on the rope that had been fastened to the little barge and thrown over to the boat he was on. It took four strong men to lift Ergeny and the chair onto the modern craft. Edith raced to the viewing area, where she immediately spotted some large fish that had come to inspect this visitor.

"Daddy, Daddy, I see blue fish and yellow fish... big ones!" She wanted him to join her to see the fish with her, but he had his attention fixed on the breathing hose and face mask Michel Ernesto was busy preparing. He'd never used a hose before, never really needing it, but he knew now the reason for the fancy boat and equipment. His heart raced in his chest, and he waved back to all of the fishing boats that had come to share the day with him. One of them held up a particularly large crab he'd harvested that morning, and Ergeny gave him an enthusiastic fist pump. That started a frenzy of showing off their respective catches, and Ergeny had to wipe his eyes a few times before Michel Ernesto called him.

"You know how to use this?" Michel called out over the breaking waves.

"I've never used one, but I think I need to stick it in my mouth and breathe through it, right?"

Michel Ernesto laughed with him. Did anyone need to teach a squirrel to climb a tree, or a polar bear to climb on a chunk of floating ice?

"Let's get you into a wet suit, then." He held up a suit he thought would fit his father.

"Nothing doing... I'm going in bare-chested. I want to feel the water." Michel Ernesto thought about protesting, but decided against it. He knew it would have been a struggle to get his father into the suit, so he gave in and started to help him undress. Edith came over to help, too. Once he was down to his boxers, Michel Ernesto handed him the mask, and swung the pivoting pulley around, with a type of swing seat attached to it. He signaled for the boat captain to maneuver them out and over the reef, and Edith screamed in delight when she saw Fidel and Ergeny Junior below them, holding their fingers over their mouths for her to keep it a secret. They lowered their anchor, and Michel Ernesto pressed the top arrow of the control, and the swing seat lifted up until Senior was seated above the edge of the boat. Another arrow and he swiveled out and over the edge, tilting the boat to the side several inches.

From below deck, Sandra climbed the steep steps with the twins. They'd been hiding there with Theresa since they'd begun the trek to the ocean in the giant wheel. Claudia and little Che were making his first boat ride, having rented it in Casilda from a friend of Michel Ernesto's. Fidel and Ergeny surfaced together on the opposite side of the boat, waiting for their father to be lowered before joining him and Michel Ernesto below. Sandra blew her father a kiss and took the controls from Michel Ernesto, so he could hop into the water with Senior. He flashed her his famous thumbs up and closed his mouth around the mouthpiece just as she let him sink below the surface. Edith ran around to the opposite side of the glass bottom, so she could spot him as he was lowered into the water. When she saw his feet enter the viewing area, she screamed her approval, and that was the brothers' signal to guide him down to his own monument in the coral.

He was surprised to see his three sons converging on him as he was lowered to the bottom, and when he looked up, he was even more surprised to see his two daughters, five grandchildren, and Claudia waving down at him, bright smiles on their faces. It looked like a picture he'd like to have on his wall. All of those beautiful faces looking down at him made him feel like he was looking up at heaven from below. He noticed Michel Ernesto look like he might be heading up for air, and signaled for him to take his hose and fill his lungs. He was sitting in the swing seat, now, just a few feet above the amazing sculpture. Fidel wiped the front of it, revealing the words, 'Ergeny lives here', and he twisted around so he could see his father reading it. Junior waved him over to see the hand-prints on the back side of it, and before any of them could stop him, Senior popped the mouthpiece out and slid off of the seat, his legs falling limply below him. Above, from the boat, a bunch of women screamed in fear that he wouldn't be able to get back to come to the surface. Senior smiled under his mask, controlling himself easily with his powerful arms, as he maneuvered himself around to where his oldest son pointed out each of the hand-prints, those of Edith and Michel Ernesto looking so tiny next to the others. Fidel gave a small kick and grabbed hold of the air line, filling his lungs again. He motioned to Junior to do the same, and he flipped his thumb up and took a deep breath. Michel Ernesto waved to the three of them, and headed for the rear of the boat, where the ladder was located. Fidel looked up and waved to Claudia and their little son, and waved to the two Ergenys that he was also going to surface. Only a minute had passed since Senior had left the hose, and he ran his fingers over every inch of the sculpture, stroking it like a cherished pet. Junior caught his attention, asking him with gestures if he wanted help getting back onto the swing. Senior signaled back for his son to head up – that he wanted a couple of minutes to himself. Ergeny knew his father was fine – he could see in his eyes he was in his element, and against the frantic

256

waving he saw from the glass screen above him, he motioned to Senior that he was heading up. He would watch from above, where he saw Fidel holding the side of the boat, in case he needed any assistance.

Now in the water alone, Ergeny took another moment to contemplate the amazing family he had only ten meters above him. Definitely worth everything he had gone through to be back with them – including spending the rest of his life in a wheelchair. He smiled again at the words 'Ergeny Lives Here', and he flashed his movie star smile at them. He had a couple of minutes left before heading to the chair and hose, but he cherished the freedom he felt in the water, on his own.

He looked off to the south through the water, knowing it was less than two kilometers away that he had held his drunken father under the water until he'd stopped struggling. "I forgive you, Dad," he said into the water, mouthing the words with his lips. He stared off in that direction for another fifteen seconds, feeling the weight of so many years of hatred and resentment lifting from his heart.

He turned again to the sculpture, and ran his index finger along the length of the diver, feeling the sharpness of the tip of the spear. "And you, too," he mouthed again, feeling the need to breathe again soon. A few strokes of his powerful arms, and he was halfway to the swing. Two bright blue fish passed in front of him as he reached for the tube. A good day to fish, he thought to himself. As he climbed onto the swing to head for the surface, a large sea turtle slipped out from a cave it had been resting in. Ergeny thought about the tires on his wheelchair, and smiled. He yanked on the hose, and the swing began its slow retreat back to the surface. His wife, five children and five grandchildren waited for him, or he might have chosen to stay.

Brian Kerr lives in Mexico with his best friend and wife Marla, their two children, his mother-in-law, two dogs, a parrot, and a few dozen budgies. When he is not writing about Cuba, he's either visiting Cuba, or cleaning out bird cages.

CPSIA information can be obtained at www.ICGtesting.com
Printed in the USA
LVOW10s1553100516

487548LV00001B/52/P